"I can gentle him, M

"I said, 'no.' "

"You didn't mean it," she said, half-surprised at her own temerity. She'd never challenged one of John Foster's orders before, but there was something about the gray that called to her, told her if she could only win his respect, his affection . . .

Her lariat snaked out suddenly, the loop settling over the horse's head. Sylvester went straight up in the air with a shriek of rage, pawing at the rope with his front hooves, flinging his head from side to side like an animal caught in a trap. As he came down, the rope hooked under one leg, Charlie darted forward to the snubbing post set into the center of the pen, racing around it, then bracing herself to take the jerk as the horse lunged forward.

Other Books by A.C. Crispin:

Yesterday's Son
V
V: East Coast Crisis (in collaboration with Howard Weinstein)
Gryphon's Eyrie (in collaboration with Andre Norton)
V: Death Tide (in collaboration with Deborah A. Marshall)

SYLVESTER

by A.C. Crispin

A TOM DOHERTY ASSOCIATES BOOK

SYLVESTER

First printing: April 1985

A TOR Book

Published by Tom Doherty Associates
8-10 West 36 Street
New York, N.Y. 10018

ISBN: 0-812-58173-3
CAN. ED.: 0-812-58174-1

Printed in the United States of America

DEDICATION

For Faith E. Treadwell, my sister, who shares with me memories of our rascally, impossible-to-catch, bullheaded and loveable chestnut gelding, Thor.

INTRODUCTION

When I was first asked to write this novelization of a film about horses and Three-Day Eventing, I accepted eagerly, thinking that since I had owned horses for twenty years, shown them, broken my current two to ride, and generally had a lot of exposure to horses and the horse world, this project would be easy.

Wrong.

I knew little to nothing about Three-Day Eventing and Combined Training when I began, but I've emerged from this book with an enormous amount of respect for the riders, trainers, and horses who compete in this thrilling, demanding, and downright risky sport. The Event horse is the triathalon champ of the equine world, required to do three extremely different things in a short space of time (one, two, or three days) and perform all of them well. And, anyone who has owned and trained horses can testify that an animal who is that athletic, mentally flexible, and physically fit is a real find.

But even rarer are the people with the ambition and determination to train and condition their horses to compete, and then ride them over those truly hair-raising cross-country courses. Anyone who saw the Eventing in the 1984 Olympics must recall the drops, water jump, and heart-stoppingly solid obstacles these horses and riders negotiated with a flair that often made it look easy.

In writing this book, I've attempted to be as accurate as possible (given the limitations of working from a screenplay in which events must necessarily be telescoped for good pacing) about the conditioning methods, training, obstacles, and work involved in Eventing. Anyone who is interested in learning more about the sport might consult:

The Complete Horse Encyclopedia compiled by Jane Kidd, Chartwell Books, Inc. The entry on Eventing provides a good overview, with lots of pictures.

Eventing Explained—A Horseman's Handbook, by Carol Green, Arco Publishing Company, Inc. A good introductory book for the experienced rider who has had little exposure to Combined Training.

Practical Eventing, by Sally O'Connor, the United States Combined Training Association.

The U.S. Combined Training Association Book of Eventing, edited by Sally O'Connor, published by Addison-Wesley Publishing Co., Inc.

Another book that is good, but rather difficult to locate, is *The Event Horse*, by Sheila Wilcox.

OR, you can write the U.S. Combined Training Association for information. Their address is: U.S. C.T.A., 292 Bridge Street, South Hamilton, MA, 01982, (617) 468-7133.

Beginning or novice riders who are tempted to try cross-country jumping at high speeds are advised to first go and watch a U. S. Combined Training Association-sponsored Event or Horse Trials, and then, if still interested, to seek the advice and coaching of an experienced trainer in the field. Falls and crashes of horse and/or rider are not uncommon. As in any other sport involving high speeds while mounted on a twelve-hundred pound horse, you *can* get hurt.

ACKNOWLEDGMENTS

I am deeply indebted to a number of individuals for their help during the writing of this book, and wish to thank them profoundly:

First and foremost, Kim U. Walnes of the U.S. Equestrian team, who, with her horse The Gray Goose, doubled for Melissa Gilbert and Sylvester in the Lexington equestrian cross-country, dressage, and jumping seen in the film. Kim spent many patient long-distance hours explaining training, conditioning, and countless other technical matters to me, as well as reading the manuscript for same. Thank you, Kim!

Esther Margolis of Newmarket Press, for helpful advice, encouragement, and a wonderful dinner at Elaine's.

Barbara B. Wheelis of the Marfa Chamber of Commerce, for all the information and questions answered about Marfa, Texas. (Which, by the way, I plan to visit soon—the people are very warm and friendly, and the climate sounds just super. I love mountains, and Marfa is smack in the middle of lots of them!)

Lucius Barre and Martha Benko of Rastar Productions, who answered my questions about Sylvester, the film, and provided many, many photos.

My husband Randy Crispin and my son, Jason Crispin, for putting up with me while I'm writing.

My mother and father, Hope and George Tickell for all those hours of babysitting.

And, last but emphatically not least, Comanche TwoBucks (Buttons) and Mr. Six Scooter (Scooter) my horses, who have given me so many good times—as well as stalls to clean!

CHAPTER 1

Charlie

The half-empty stock truck lurched as it turned off U. S. 67 onto the narrow section road. Inside the truck, the rawboned gray gelding fought to keep his feet as he and the other horses crashed against each other and the metal sides of the vehicle. One horse, a rangy paint mare, had already fallen and been stepped on, barely managing to regain her feet before being trampled. Her left leg was bleeding.

The gray skidded again on the manure-covered floor as the driver hauled the truck into a hard left turn, gears clashing in protest. Eyes wide with terror, the gelding fought to stay up, his lean but powerful hindquarters sending his unshod hooves scrabbling for purchase on the greasy metal surface of the trailer bed. Another horse went down with a thud, but something in the big gray—some sense of balance, of timing, plus a stubborn determination—kept him from giving in, and, finally, when the truck stopped with a last heave and jerk, the gelding was still standing, legs braced.

The horse flicked forward his black-flecked ears as he heard shouts, then he pinned them back against his head as human boots rang on the metal side rails of the trailer. The rear gate of the truck opened with a crash and the horses began milling within, scenting water yet leery of the sharp downward slope of the ramp.

"Hey, you! Getalong now!" A rope snapped against the gelding's dirt-crusted rump and he snaked his head warningly, his tail wringing from side to side as he tensed to kick. Another snap of the rope sent him plunging forward, toward the ramp. As his forehooves touched its wooden surface, however, he turned sharply to the left, leaping down the six foot drop to the hard ground of the corral.

Landing sent a violent jar through his undernourished body, but at least he was free of the hated truck. The gray gelding hesitated, tempted to join the other horses who were now bunched near the water trough on the other side of the corral; but a ewe-necked sorrel bared her teeth at him warningly, and he held off, standing by himself on the opposite side of the area.

He was exhausted; he hurt. All around him was the hated smell of men, and memories flooded his mind as his nostrils flared . . . memories of the bucking saddle chafing his tender back, the flank strap pinching his loins as he reared and sunfished, fighting with the two-legged enemy who clung shrieking to his back, while the roar of the crowd rose all around him. These bad memories almost completely overlaid any earlier ones now—fuzzy recollections of a different kind of human, one who had a softer voice and kind hands, who had taken him for rides along quiet roads and across gray-green prairies. A kind of human with a different scent . . .

The gray raised his head and nickered softly as a faint, almost-familiar odor crossed his nostrils.

"Hey, lookit that, Charlie! You've made a conquest! That ugly fleabitten ol' thing's in love with you, I swear! Didja see him talkin' to you?"

Charlene Railsberg glared over at "Red" Adams. "Stick it, Red. That horse has more brains than you do." She looked back over the fence rail of the holding pen at the homely looking, longbacked gray gelding. His lower lip hung down like a sulky kid's, reminding Charlie of her little brother Seth when she refused to give him money to play the video game in the office at their trailer park. The animal's coat was harsh and filthy, and she could barely make out the small patches of darker gray that speckled it.

Slowly the gelding turned his head to look at her. Charlie chirruped encouragingly, hardly knowing why she was bothering, only to have the horse flatten his ears, then turn his rump to her, his tail swishing warningly.

"Hoo, boy! Looks like you've finally met someone even nastier than you, Rail," Red chortled.

Charlie bristled at the hated nickname. At sixteen, she was still short and slight, barely beginning to fill out her double-A bras. Not deigning to reply to Red's jibe, she hopped down from the fence to go back to work. Picking up the reins of the compact Appaloosa who stood ground-tied near the biggest of the stockyard's barns, she swung into her worn Western saddle. The short-coupled little horse danced as he felt her weight, then quieted as she spoke to him firmly. "Hey, cut it out, Appy. You're a stock horse now, not a bronc.'' Charlie absently patted the pony's black-spotted shoulder, turning back once more to look back at the ugly gray. There was something about him . . . something . . .

''Hey, Rail, you gonna sit there all day and moon over your new honey? Foster's paying us to *work.*'' With a sudden hiss, Red's bullwhip sang over Charlie's head, snaking her beat-up old Stetson off her head, sending it spinning into the high-fenced corral, causing a general panic as the broncs raced around the pen. Charlie watched helplessly as her favorite headgear was trampled to unrecognizability. And she couldn't spare the money for a new hat.

She turned back to Red. ''That was a stinking thing to do, you lousy—!''

He grinned nastily. ''Sorry, Charlie . . .''

As she stared at his freckled dusty face two years' worth of taunts, nasty tricks and practical jokes rose up in her memory—and something snapped. With a wordless yell of rage, Charlie spurred Appy straight at the other wrangler, grabbing at his head with a vague idea of appropriating his hat. *Red* had parents who'd buy him another—that was most of the problem, they had never refused him anything. Adams reined his bay around so sharply that it reared in pain, and his bullwhip lashed against Appy's rump. ''Stop that!'' she yelled, grabbing at his reins as the horses crashed together. He pulled back just as she shoved, and both riders lost their balance and tumbled off into the Texas dust, still fighting.

Charlie dug a knee into Red's chest, still grabbing for his hat, then gasped as he caught her wrist and twisted it.

She yelped, punching him viciously in the stomach, then aimed another blow at his groin—

"Stop it!" A hand clamped on the back of Charlie's neck, hooked into the bandanna she wore, and dragged her back, away from Adams. Charlie looked up through a haze of sweat and fury to see her boss, John Foster, the owner of the stockyards. The old man gave her another shake, glaring from her to Red. "I'll see you both in my office at six. Until then, Red, clean the horse troughs. Charlie, check the fences up on the mesa. Now get back to work!"

Dropping Charlie as though she were a rag doll, Foster strode away. The young woman stood staring after him, her throat tight with fear and dismay. She'd never seen Foster so furious since the time that Red had forgotten to water the steers and one of them had collapsed from heat exhaustion. Charlie, Foster and Dr. Mathis had been up all night and the Hereford had nearly died.

She turned to look back at Red Adams, who was slowly climbing to his feet, his lanky seventeen-year-old frame streaked and muddy from sweat and dust. His pale blue eyes were flat as he looked down at her. "I'll get you for that, Rail," he said, and his low, inflectionless voice was even more threatening than his words.

Charlie turned away and retrieved her horse, sending the Appaloosa jogging toward the ancient, green-encroached butte marking the boundary of Foster's land. He leased the pasture to Clint Perry, and it had been several days since anyone had checked the fences—Foster had given her the preferred chore, making Charlie hope that he'd seen Red swipe her hat. Riding the mesa would be a good chance to get away from the yard with its dust, doomed fat cattle, and thin-flanked horses.

Charlie chewed fretfully at her lower lip, remembering the look in Red's eyes. Before this the wrangler had regarded her as just another hand to be tormented, just as he did Peter, the mildly retarded boy who mucked the stables, and Tommy John, the Indian who, along with Adams, broke the rank horses. But now the redhead's expression warned her that from now on, she, Charlene Railsberg, was to be singled out for genuine hate.

She sighed deeply, causing Appy to flick back his ears at her. Charlie smiled faintly as she patted the black-spotted neck. "Don't rile yourself, pal. *I'm* the one in trouble, not you. You've turned into a real prize, Appy." She wondered how much longer Foster would keep the little Appaloosa around. Now that he could rein, cut, and head a calf, the sensible thing would be to sell him. Charlie would be glad to see him get a good home—the little horse deserved it, after working hard for nearly two years to go from a raw bronc to a reliable, "finished" stock horse, but she knew she'd miss him terribly.

Just once, she thought miserably, *I wish I didn't have to train them, then say goodbye. I wish I could hang on to one of the good ones.*

Charlene Railsberg had been riding since she was eight, and working part-time for John Foster since she was twelve, but had never had a horse of her own. Her father, Charles Railsberg, had been a truck driver—when he wasn't drinking, that is. He and his wife, Lena, had been killed nearly two years before when his sedan tore out the guard-rail on the Sibilo Creek bridge, plunging into Sibilo Creek, deep and swollen with a heavy spring rain.

Charlie, as the oldest of their three children, had struggled to finish high school while working at the stockyards part-time as a wrangler. At first Lena's twenty-six-year-old cousin, Thelma, had lived with them in their tiny trailer, but last year she'd gotten married and moved to Oklahoma, leaving Charlie to care for and support her two brothers, Grant, ten, and Seth, five.

Those months had been the worst. Some evenings after a day of school, work, cooking and laundry, Charlie had been so exhausted by the time she put the boys to bed that she'd had to set her alarm for 5:00 a.m. so she could get up and do her homework assignments.

After taking full course loads each summer for two years, Charlie had managed to graduate from high school a year ahead of her class. She hadn't been a candidate for *magna cum laude,* but she hadn't had the lowest average, either. She remembered the day she'd reported to the principal's office to pick up her diploma, and the way Mr. Monroe had shaken her hand and told her he admired her. Sometimes, when things seemed overwhelming, Charlie thought about that moment, holding it in her mind as a small secret source of strength. But mostly her graduation had been important because it meant she could work full time.

It was certainly easier now than it had been in those days. Memories flooded Charlie's mind as she rode the barbed-wire fences, her eyes mechanically checking for any breaks or weak points. As she recalled those eighteen months of never-ending work, she found herself praying that Foster wouldn't fire her, now, just when things had begun to get a little better.

Foster paid her four dollars an hour, good wages for a wrangler, and with the two hundred-dollar check each month from her father's insurance—a benefit due to run out in six months—she and the boys had been able to afford hamburger for dinner a couple of times a week, now, and sometimes a roast chicken on Sundays. Charlie had been able to buy the boys new clothes, as well as put nearly three hundred dollars into a "rainy day" savings account at the Marfa National Bank.

Her blue-gray eyes narrowed as they fixed on a sagging fence post, and she swung off Appy, reaching into her saddlebag for her gloves, wire cutters, hammer, nails and extra wire. Tufts of reddish hair clung to the barbed wire, where one of the steers had tried to reach through for a particularly appealing clump of grass on the other side of the fence. Throwing her hundred and nine pounds against the post, Charlie managed to straighten it, then, after tightening the sagging strands of wire, pounded it back into the ground. The temporary repair would hold for a few days, but the post would have to be replaced.

When she had checked her watch after remounting, she set Appy to a jogtrot, checking the remainder of the fence line as quickly as possible. It was 5:15 and by now she was several miles from the stockyard. She'd have to hurry.

Red Adams was already in Foster's office when Charlie opened the door; he stared flatly at her over the rim of the beer he was drinking. John Foster was on the telephone and did not look up. Charlie sat down in the chair next to his desk so she wouldn't have to look at Red.

She glanced over at Foster, studying him covertly as he talked. At sixty-three, his tall frame remained unbent, but deep wrinkles had settled around his blue eyes, traveled down his cheeks, seaming his once-fair but now weather-beaten skin into a sheet of aging parchment. His wispy white hair, now beginning to recede, was a huge contrast to the luxuriant moustache bracketing his upper lip.

Foster's eyes slid sideways and Charlie, with a guilty start, hastily shifted her gaze. His office was a small room that had been tacked onto the top of the auction building. Late afternoon sunlight shafted through the grimy window, lighting up the even dirtier glass on the old trophy case filled with tarnished silver and faded rosettes. Above the case hung twenty or thirty framed black-and-whites of Foster, on horseback, in uniform. An antique saber and 7th Army Cavalry patch completed the memorabilia wall.

The rest of the office was taken up with sagging vinyl couches, and the cracked leather chair Charlie sat on. Stacks of *Practical Horseman, Western Horseman, The Cattleman's Journal*, and *Equus* dominated every flat space except the top of Foster's desk, which was the only empty surface in the room.

Foster, still on the telephone, made a sound of exasperation. "We can accommodate you up to sixty head, if you gotta sell, Marion, but the prices are bad now, just about as bad as they're gonna be all summer." He listened for a second, reaching for his pipe, then shook his head without completing the gesture. "No, that's not what I said, Marion. What I said was, if you have the grass, for the luvva Pete keep 'em on the grass till things get better!"

Charlie reached for an issue of *Practical Horseman* and opened it to an article on dressage. She gazed fascinated at the pictures of the beautiful sleek horses with their tophatted riders, walking, trotting with their necks arched and their noses pointing directly toward the ground and their strides so long they seemed to float, moving sideways as though they danced on air, effortlessly. Dressage, she knew, was the discipline—the art, really—of training the horse and rider to reach the peak of sensitivity, control, and balance as they performed specified tests demanding work at the walk, the trot, and the canter, as well as more specialized movements such as the half-pass and the pirouette. For a moment Charlie imagined herself as one of those serene, concentrating riders, then was jerked out of her reverie by the sound of Foster banging the phone back into its cradle.

Reaching for his pipe, he began to fill it, his eyes traveling slowly from Charlie to Red. "You'll make minimum or less working for any of the other outfts around here, even if they'd hire you. Which," he snapped his lighter and puffed the pipe to life, "they wouldn't. Remember that you're underage."

Red made a rude noise. "Cut the crap. You need us to break the rodeo stock, Foster. Peter sure can't, Tommy John's so wild himself that he's just as apt to ruin a horse as break him. There's two people can break horses around here and do it right. Me and her." He jerked his chin at Charlie without looking at her.

"And him," Charlie said, indicating Foster. "He's forgotten more about horses than we'll probably ever know."

"Speak for yourself, Rail," Red snapped. "Besides, he doesn't have time."

"What I don't have time for," Foster broke in, "is a couple of kids who act like they never left the sandbox stage. Now I want you to shake hands and apologize."

Charlie stiffened. The bare thought of touching Red repulsed her. "All right, Mr. Foster," she said, after a long moment, "but I'm warning him right now, if he touches me or my horse again with that whip of his, I'm gonna shove it up—"

"That's enough, Charlie," Foster said.

Red snickered. "Oh, macho, Rail, macho."

"Take a good look then. You'll never see it in a mirror, will you, Red?" Charlie taunted.

The lanky wrangler came up off the battered vinyl couch like a lunging bronc, and Charlie took an involuntary step backward. *"That's enough!"* Foster bellowed, and Adams halted.

The stockyard owner slammed his pipe down on his desk, then looked down in even greater disgust as the stem broke in his hand. "That's it! You're both on suspension. I've had enough of you two! Any more fighting or dirty tricks, you're both fired, and I'll send the rodeo stock to the killers from now on. Life's too short. Now get out of here."

Charlie walked wearily to her ancient Ford pickup and pulled herself up into the cab, feeling as though Foster had literally chewed her up, then spit her out. How the heck was she supposed to keep Red from harassing her so that *she* wouldn't get fired, too? She started the engine, realizing glumly that her gas gauge was again resting on "E," and she had exactly . . . a dollar thirty-four. Charlie slammed the Ford into gear, then turned out of the stockyard without looking back. The pickup's engine knocked and sputtered so loudly she didn't hear the homely gray gelding's faint nicker . . .

CHAPTER 2

Matt

Charlie wheeled her pickup past the Presidio County Courthouse, drove across the square with its Chinese elms and boarded-up stores, and turned into Webb's gas station with a sigh of relief. Places out here in the westernmost portion of Texas were so spread out that she'd been driving with a wary eye on the gas gauge, fingers crossed that she wouldn't end up stranded on the road east of town. Not that she'd have to worry; sooner or later someone she knew would come along: in Marfa, Texas, everyone knew everyone else for miles around. But she didn't want to be any later than necessary getting home to the boys.

Pulling her solitary dollar out of her jeans, she started to climb out of the cab, then sat back grinning as the proprietor came around the corner of the station, and, seeing her, started over. Resting her chin on her arm, the lone dollar between her teeth, Charlie waited.

Matt Grey was nineteen, slim and tough as a mustang,

with regular features, black hair combed off his forehead and the darkest eyes she'd ever seen. With his white tee-shirt and battered jeans, he looked like someone from a scene out of "Rebel Without A Cause," a film they'd watched together one night at the drive-in in Alpine.

"You crazy—" he grinned at her as he plucked the bill out of her mouth. "You get crazier all the time, Charlie."

Matt stuffed the limp single into his pocket as he unhooked the hose and began pumping the gas. Charlie shrugged. "What's new with you?"

"Nothin' ever changes around here," he said. "What's new with *you?*"

"Mr. Foster got some rodeo horses in today, Matt. There's a gray one looks just like Sylvester Stallone. Droopy lower lip and all."

"Oh yeah?" he hung up the hose, shaking his head. "What're you gonna do with him, teach him to box?"

"No, but I think I'll ask Foster to let me try breaking him."

"You could get hurt," he protested. "You're gettin' too old for this stuff now." Exasperation tinged his pleasant baritone. "When are you gonna quit playing with horses?"

This was an old argument, and she grinned cheekily at him. "When horses quit being more interesting than people."

A slow grin spread over his face, revealing straight white teeth, then he wiggled his eyebrows suggestively. "Come play with me, instead."

Charlie snorted, then, in spite of herself, began to laugh. "I'm serious now," Matt protested, and she fell silent. "I'm gettin' tired of waiting."

She didn't look at him as she started the old Ford.

"Then don't, Matt. I never said for you to wait." Without a backward glance she threw the pickup into gear and pulled out. She turned onto the street, aware without knowing how she knew that Matt Grey was standing there beside the gas pumps, watching her go. "Doggone it, Matt," she mumbled unhappily, "quit pushing me. I have enough to worry about without getting involved with you."

Charlie glanced down at the gas gauge as she drove, and her lips tightened as she saw that, instead of a dollar's worth, Matt had pumped in half a tank.

Ten minutes later, she turned off a road at the edge of town, behind another stand of Chinese elms. A battered sign greeted her, as it did every day. "Happy Trails Park—Day–Week–Month Rent, Lease, Sales, Playground, Full Hook-ups," it read. Home was the sagging gold and white Schultz two-bedroom parked on the end lot. Charlie parked the Ford and hopped out, feeling weariness flood over her like water. *Getting old, Charlene,* she thought, stretching with one hand on the small of her back.

The front door of the Schultz banged open, and two boys bounced down the stairs. "Hi, Charlie!"

She lengthened her strides toward them. "Hi, Grant, hi, Seth! Did you take the hamburger out so it could thaw?"

Grant, who at ten resented any inference that he wasn't completely infallible, looked disgusted. "Of *course* I did," he said. He was a tall, sturdy boy, with hair even darker than his sister's, though his eyes were brown. Seth, the five-year-old, would look exactly like him in five years. Charlie kissed the little boy's rounded cheek, then ruffed Grant's hair.

"Where's Mrs. Stewart?" she asked as they went up the steps into the trailer's ten-by-ten living room. Charlie sank into the rickety couch, feeling her bones wanting to continue on through the sagging upholstery.

"She had to go at six," Grant said. "She said she had to start supper for her own kids."

Charlie frowned. "I pay her to watch you," she said, sighing with relief as Grant pulled one sun-baked needle-nosed Western boot off, then helped Seth with the other. She wriggled her toes, clad in bright red knee socks. "She should've taken you over to her place if she had to go."

"You were late tonight, Charlie," Seth said, staring at her solemnly. "Why? Grant and me was worried."

"We got a load of rodeo horses in, and then I had to get gas," she explained, hoisting herself off the couch determinedly.

"You see Matt?" Grant asked, his dark eyes suddenly sharp.

"None of your business," Charlie snapped. "I'm going to grab a quick shower. Grant, you put the hamburger on to brown, and cut up a couple of carrots. Peel up those potatoes, too."

When she returned from the bathroom, wearing an ancient tee-shirt that hung to her knees, her short hair toweled-dry and wisping around her face, the smell of the beef made her stomach grumble. Hastily, Charlie chopped two onions, mixed them in with the beef and vegetables, then sprinkled flour, salt and pepper into the saucepan. Covering it, she turned away from the stove in time to catch Grant examining a livid bruise on his shoulder. "What happened?" she asked. "Grant, were you fighting again?"

He nodded matter-of-factly. "Why?" She held his gaze

sternly. "I don't mind fighting if it's for a good reason, but if you were bullying—"

"Ben Daniels is older n' bigger than me," Grant interrupted sullenly, his freckled features darkening. "But I fixed him good. He'll never say *that* 'bout us again!"

"Say what?"

"That Seth and me belong in the Boy's Camp. That his mom said since she works for the courthouse she could take us away and put us in an orphanage."

Charlie's mouth thinned. "Over my dead body." Turning back to the saucepan, she stirred the stew vigorously, adding a shake of garlic, a pinch of sage. *I'd like to pinch Mrs. Daniels's neck,* she thought viciously. *That biddy's got no right to say things like that where her kid could overhear them and torment Grant and Seth like that.*

"What's an orphan?" Seth asked, tugging at her shirt.

"Somebody who doesn't have any mom or dad, honey," Charlie said, as gently as she could. "Grant, set the table, please."

"Are we oprhans?"

"No, Seth, we're a family. Get your booster seat. It's almost time to eat."

After emptying a package of frozen peas into the saucepan and stirring them until they were tender, Charlie added a few drops of Kitchen Bouquet to the gravy, then began dishing up the stew. "Grant, pour the milk."

They all sat down at the table, noses twitching at the smell of food. "Whose turn is it?" Charlie asked.

"Grant's," Seth said.

They tipped their heads as Grant began to speak. "Dear Lord, please bless this food to our use. Say hi to Mom and Dad, and bring me a twelve gauge if you can. Amen."

Forks clattered on the faded yellow plastic plates as the Railsbergs began to eat.

"The Indian boy sat astride his pinto colt, watching the braves thunder along beside the buffalo herd. His colt danced beneath him as the ground trembled from the hooves of the shaggy brown buffalo, and Little Hawk patted his shoulder. 'Soon, my friend, soon,' he told his pinto. 'We will hunt together, you and I. The chief, my father, has promised it will not be much longer.' " Charlie looked up from the pages of *Little Hawk of the Cheyenne* to see Seth blink rapidly, fighting sleep.

"You're tired, honey," she said, closing the book. "We'll finish it tomorrow."

"Okay, Charlie," he said, fighting a yawn as she settled him into his bed. Kissing him good night, she turned in the miniscule bedroom to see Grant, without being told, put his *Hardy Boys* library book down. "Good night, you guys," she said, her hand on the light switch.

"G'night, Charlie."

She made her way along the moonlit hall of the trailer, her fingers running along the plaster-board paneled walls, her eyes so heavy she was tempted to forget about brushing her teeth, just this once. But force of habit won out, and, a few minutes later, Charlie crawled into the rickety double bed that had been her parents', her mouth tingling with the taste of Crest gel. She relaxed, her eyes focusing sleepily on the moonlit horse photos she'd cut out of *Practical Horseman* issues and stuck in dime-store frames. Pictures of dressage horses, jumping horses, roping horses, steeplechasers, horses working, horses playing, horses dancing on air . . .

Charlene Railsberg drifted toward sleep to the imaginary drum of pounding hooves, visions of galloping, jumping, plunging horses surrounding her. And in the lead was the big fleabitten gray with the droopy lip, the one she had already begun to think of as Sylvester.

"Can I break the big gray, Mr. Foster?" Charlie looked over at the stockyards owner as he stood beside her gazing over the top rail of the rodeo horses' pen. The rangy long-backed gray was still ostracized from the rest of the bunch, standing by himself on the opposite side of the corral, his ears back, his teeth bared at any challenger.

"I don't think so, Charlie," Foster replied, his pale blue eyes studying the animal in question. "Something tells me he could be a real ugly customer. I've seen that look before, on real rank broncs. That one might *try* t'hurt you on purpose. I'm wondering if maybe I shouldn't take him on myself."

Charlie bit her lip in disappointment, but was inwardly relieved that at least Foster hadn't mentioned turning the gray over to Red. The lanky wrangler took pleasure in brutalizing the spirit out of any horse that showed signs of being a fighter, and instinctively she knew that the big gray would fight—and fight hard.

She laughed suddenly as the horse relaxed slightly, allowing his lower lip to droop. "I call him Sylvester Stallone," she said. "Hey, Sylvester!"

The horse turned toward her, his ears coming forward, his expression changing so radically that he looked like a different animal for a second. He nickered, rumbling low in his throat, the sound a horse uses for someone he likes, someone who feeds him. "Hey, look at that!" Charlie exclaimed. "I think he likes me! Maybe he likes women better than men!"

Swinging a leg over the top rail, she dropped into the bronc pen, her lariat in her hand. Foster's voice came from behind her. "Take the buckskin, honey. He'll make a good cowhorse after some training and we put a couple hundred pounds on him."

Never taking her eyes from the big, thin-flanked gray, Charlie began to swing her rope, the loop growing as she paid out the coil. Foster raised his voice from behind her. "Charlie? Did you hear me? Take the buckskin!"

"I heard you," she said, still watching Sylvester as he backed away, his ears again flattened, his eyes glaring once more. "I can gentle him, Mr. Foster."

"I said, 'no.' "

"You didn't mean it," she said, half-surprised at her own temerity. She'd never challenged one of John Foster's orders before, but there was something about the gray that called to her, told her if she could only win his respect, his affection . . .

Her lariat snaked out suddenly, the loop settling over the horse's head. Sylvester went straight up in the air with a shriek of rage, pawing at the rope with his front hooves, flinging his head from side to side like an animal caught in a trap. As he came down, the rope hooked under one leg, Charlie darted forward to the snubbing post set into the center of the pen, racing around it, then bracing herself to take the jerk as the horse lunged forward.

When Sylvester reached the end of the slack, his momentum flipped him sideways and he fell heavily onto the packed dirt of the corral. Charlie took advantage of the moment's respite to tighten the rope several times around the post, keeping hold of the bight. The gray horse lay still for only a second, then he was up again, this time charging straight for the young woman.

Charlie scuttled around the post, keeping the rope tight, and Sylvester fell again. "Stubborn, aren't you?" she mumbled, taking up on the snub, watching the animal's thin sides heave. Being thrown down is the most disconcerting thing that can happen to a horse, and tends to take much of the fight out of them. But Sylvester had fallen twice, and still showed no signs of backing off.

Within a second he was up again, charging, and this time Charlie took up so much slack that he was trapped, nose nearly bumping the post, his eyes bulging as the lariat cut off his air. "Take it easy," she soothed, moving toward him. "You don't want to choke yourself, dummy. Quiet down a little, and let me loosen that rope." Carefully she reached for the sweaty, mud-streaked neck, where the lariat dug into the animal's straining windpipe. "Just give me a second and I'll get this loosened up, Sylvester. Take it easy—"

As she moved to loosen the lariat, the gray swung his head around like a snake, stained ivory teeth flashing wickedly. She gasped as he grabbed her hand, ripping the skin. With her left fist, Charlie punched the animal's muzzle, forcing him to let go, just as Foster jerked on the rope from the other side.

"Charlie!" He reached for her torn hand. "Let me see that. How bad did he get you?"

Charlie hardly felt the pain, mesmerized as she was by the undaunted fury in the big gray's eyes. "He's not scared," she breathed, as Foster wiggled her fingers, sighing when he realized nothing was broken. "Look at that,

Mr. Foster. He can't hardly breathe, and he's still not afraid of us. He's got a lot of guts, doesn't he?''

''Too much,'' her boss said curtly, unsnubbing the rope from the post, and, with an expert flick of his fingers, releasing Sylvester. ''Red's breaking him. He's too rank.''

''No!'' Charlie cried. ''You can't!''

''Come on, let's get out of here.'' Foster helped her over the fence, walking quickly toward his office. ''We want to get ice on that hand. When was the last time you had a tetanus shot?''

''This winter, when I stepped on that pitchfork Peter left lying around,'' she responded automatically, then looked at him beseechingly. ''Please, Mr. Foster! Don't do this. I know I can gentle him!''

''If that snake kills Red, I've done the world a favor. On the other hand, if he kills you, I'd wind up stuck with your baby brothers, and I'm done with raising kids. No way, Charlie.''

''There isn't a horse alive I can't gentle, Mr. Foster. You know that!''

''Yeah, maybe so, Charlie, but there's some horses that aren't worth the bother, and that gray's one of 'em. Some horses are just bad, they're not honest, you can't ever trust 'em. They're like criminals, they've got something inside that's missing. They're like those people who can't tell right from wrong . . . what do they call 'em? Sociopaths.''

''But—'' she stared at him frantically. ''Didn't you *see* how he used his hocks? He's got natural balance, a lot of spring there. He can coil up and let loose like he was born to it! I bet he'd make a great cutting horse!''

''He's too big for a cutting horse. That horse is Red's, end of story, period.'' As she opened her mouth to argue again, his mouth tightened. "I said, end of discussion! Now get some ice on that hand, get it bandaged, then get back to work!"

Charlie's voice was low, dangerous. "Fire me, Mr. Foster. I'm aggravating you. You said that if we aggravated you, we'd get fired. Well, go ahead. I don't want to work for a fool, and only a fool would give a horse like that to Red to be ruined."

Her boss stared at her for a long, furious moment, then turned abruptly and strode away. Charlie stood looking after him, biting her lip, shaking, fighting hard not to cry.

"What happened to your hand, Charlie?" Seth asked, staring dismayed at the blood-crusted gauze bandage as his sister, wincing, peeled it away from her fingers.

"Sylvester bit me," she said, flexing the injury cautiously. "But I'm okay."

"Here," Grant said, bringing over a bowl of ice cubes bobbing in water. "You'd better soak it. Did you take an aspirin?"

"I'm fine," she said, breath hissing between her teeth as she lowered the hand into the bowl. "I had an ice pack on it earlier for almost an hour."

"Who's Sylvester?" Seth wanted to know.

"A big gray horse Mr. Foster got in yesterday. I roped him, but he's a fighter. Then," she stared glumly into the pinkening water, "he gave him to Red to break. Makes me sick to think about what Red might do. Then I went and made things worse when I told Mr. Foster he was a fool. That's the first time I ever yelled at him, and I feel bad about it. If it weren't for him, you kids would be in the Boys' Camp, and I'd be bagging groceries somewhere."

"He'll forgive you, Charlie," Grant said. "He knows how you feel about him."

"Yeah . . . but what's going to happen to Sylvester?"

"Sounds like he's too mean to bother with," Grant said, stirring milk and butter into the macaroni and cheese mix. "Seth, set the table."

"I think that horse is fighting because he's scared, not mean," Charlie said. "A couple of times he's looked at me like—I don't know—like he's appealing to me, or something. To save him."

"Sounds like you're getting all gushy about a bronc," Grant said. "You always told me and Seth that people who get all gushy about horses and try to treat them like big pets only get hurt. Now look at you."

"Maybe you're right," she sighed, "but this horse doesn't strike me as the kind that's really bad, the way some of 'em are. He's different—"

"Let's go see him," Seth said, carrying the salt and pepper shakers over from the counter. "After supper."

"Who? Matt?" Grant ignored his sister's glare. "Mr. Foster?"

"No, dummy." Seth looked as exasperated as only a five-year-old can. "Sylvester."

"It's night," Grant said. "You can't look at horses at night."

"We could bring him some carrots," Seth said. "Maybe then he'd be nicer."

"Yeah, then *you'd* be the one with the messed-up hand. I think we ought to go get ice cream, instead. We could pick up Matt." He glanced over at his sister as he began ladling out dollops of macaroni and cheese onto the plates. "How about it, Charlie?"

"Okay to the ice cream," she said shortly. "No to Matt."

"Why don't you like him?" Grant asked quietly. "He's a neat guy. There are always girls hanging around Webb's just to talk to him."

Charlie took her hand out of the water, drying it on a paper towel before dumping the remaining ice and water into the chipped porcelain sink. "I like him okay, I guess," she said softly, looking out the window of the trailer to the hard-packed dirt road beyond. "But right now I gotta concentrate on raising you guys. If I think about anything else, I feel like I'll just fly apart into a million pieces. You know what I mean?"

Grant took a plate out of the refrigerator with cut-up carrot and celery sticks. "I guess so."

"Matt likes *you*," Seth said. "He told me and Grant so."

Charlie sighed. "Eat your dinner, Seth."

CHAPTER 3

Red's Revenge

Matt Grey was sweeping out the office of his gas station when he saw a familiar battered Ford pickup pull up beside his pumps. He approached the vehicle warily, seeing that Charlie's hand was bandaged as it rested on the steering wheel. She'd hurt herself again. Matt grimaced. Charlie stared straight at him, daring him to say something.

Grant, sitting beside his sister, waved. "We're going for ice cream after awhile, Matt, wanna come?"

"Sure," Matt said.

At the same moment, Charlie said, "He's busy, Grant, can't you see?" She faltered to a halt, biting her lip.

Seth leaned across his brother. "We're gonna go see a horse that's got *big* teeth!"

Matt made a face. "I'll bet. That where you got the war wound, Charlie?"

"She's okay," Grant said. "Come on."

"Okay," Matt said, grinning wryly. "*Is* that the same horse you were talking about yesterday?"

"Yeah," Charlie said shortly. "Mr. Foster assigned him to Red today. I want to make sure he's all right."

"Sounds like he and Red will make a perfect couple." She started the truck. "Sounds like you're as bad as he is."

Hastily, Matt jumped into the cab of the pickup. Grant grinned at him. "I got four dollars collecting aluminum cans. I'm buying the ice cream."

"Great," Matt said, "thanks, pal."

Charlie turned around in the driver's seat. "Aren't you gonna lock up? Your uncle Webb would turn over in his grave if you went running off and left his place wide open."

Matt eyed her measuringly, then grinned. "Grant, go lock up. If I get out, she's gonna take off."

Grant slithered out of the truck, laughing.

The Ford turned into the stockyards, then slewed around so its headlights shone into the corral where the rodeo stock milled nervously, agitated by the sudden, harsh illumination. Charlie leaned forward, her eyes searching the horses. Paints, bays, chestnuts, a roan Appaloosa . . . but no gray.

"Which one is Sylvester?" Matt asked.

"He isn't here," Charlie said, forcing words past the tightness in her jaw and throat. *Where is he? What did Red do?*

She turned the wheel, driving slowly in a circle, her eyes probing the night. Finally, Charlie spotted a light-colored hide in one of the small breaking pens, and drove over toward it.

"Oh, no!" she whispered, as the high beams picked out the rawboned gray gelding

Sylvester stood by the fence, his coat stiff with dried lather and mud, his flanks even more sunken than when he'd arrived. Spur tracks raced along his sides, and welts scored his head and face. His mouth was torn at the corners from a Mexican spade bit Red liked to inflict on really rough performers.

"I guess Red rode him," Matt said, sounding dismayed.

"Look, Charlie," Grant said. "He doesn't even have any water in there, and it was another hot one today. We'd better get him some."

"Yeah," Charlie breathed, heading for a bucket near the auction barn.

"Let me," Matt said, taking it from her. "Your hand."

Charlie walked back over to the fence, only to find Sylvester glaring at her in the headlights, his ears pinned back. "Poor guy," she said. "He really worked you over, didn't he?" Slowly, talking to the gelding, she climbed over the fence. A minute later, Matt was back with the water. He climbed awkwardly over the gate as Charlie steadied the bucket, then lowered it to the ground and climbed back over the fence.

Charlie picked up the slopping container and started across the pen to Sylvester, talking softly all the while.

"Charlie, don't be crazy!" Matt hissed from outside the fence. "He won't drink with you there, and you might get hurt!"

"Shut up," she said, advancing slowly, one boot toe only an inch or so in front of the other, moving at a snail's glide. "Take it easy, Sylvester. Come on, here's the water. I know you're so thirsty . . ."

She continued to talk softly to the horse, watching his nostrils widen as he scented the water. Finally she stopped about four feet from his nose. "You're going to have to come the rest of the way, Sylvester," she said. "C'mon, nobody's gonna hurt you . . ."

The big gray tossed his head, his eyes hard and wary, his ears pinned. Slowly he edged forward, pushing his nose toward the water. He curled his lip over the rim, touched it, then jerked back, shying as it sloshed. "Come on," breathed Charlie. "It's okay . . ." She whistled softly between her teeth, never moving.

Sylvester tossed his head, took two more cautious steps forward—

—and then his head was in the bucket, and his loud slurping swallows dominated the still night air. The hollows above his eyes pulsed as he drank greedily. Charlie turned her head, smiling in triumph, to see Seth, grinning, wave his clasped hands over his head like a victorious fighter. Matt, an arm hooked over Grant's shoulders, grinned ruefully at her.

"Big deal," he said, but Charlie could tell he was impressed. Grant nodded, giving her a "thumbs up" signal.

Sylvester drained the bucket, then looked hopefully at Charlie for more. Carefully, she reached out, managed to draw her bandaged fingers along his neck before he stepped away.

"Matt," she called, "get me another bucket, okay?"

A minute later he was back, another full bucket in his hand. Charlie put it down at her feet, and, after an eye-rolling moment, Sylvester approached, began drinking. She stroked his shoulder gently, murmuring softly as she did so.

Matt's voice came from behind her. "Somehow I thought he'd be better looking, to impress you like that."

Charlie laughed, feeling triumphant as she stroked the animal's strong, well-defined withers. "He's better looking than you are."

"Now I *know* you've got rocks in your head," he retorted.

After Sylvester had finished the second bucket, he retreated once more to his corner, but Charlie knew that the ice had definitely been broken. And during the moments when she'd stroked his side, she'd discovered something important: the faint scar of an old girth gall. At one time, Sylvester had been broken to ride. It was fear that had soured him on humans, not inborn meanness. If she could teach him to trust again . . .

Gathering up the buckets, Charlie climbed back over the fence. Matt met her on the other side, silently taking one of the pails. They hung them back in the corner of the barn, feeling their way in the darkness, then Charlie turned back toward her pickup and the boys—only to bump into Matt.

His arms came up to encircle her, pull her close, and he bent his head, his mouth seeking hers. For just a second Charlie leaned against him, her lips warm beneath his, then she stiffened and pulled away. "Let me go, Matt!"

His breathing was a little fast, as though he'd just been running. "Why? You liked it as much as I did. I could tell."

"You keep pushing me, Matt!" Charlie walked around his tall shadow in the dark, staying far out of his reach. There was something treacherous in her mind, her body, that wanted to give in, hold him, and that was something she couldn't succumb to; she had Grant and Seth to think about. "I want you to stop it, or, so help me, I won't come within ten miles of you."

"Charlie," his voice held a strange mixture of resentment and sadness. "You keep stonewalling me. You know I care—"

"I know," she said tightly, leaning over to pick up a thick section of alfalfa. "And I don't want you to care."

"That's because you're afraid that maybe if you knock down some of that wall, that you might end up having to admit you care about me."

Charlie didn't answer as she walked out of the barn, past Sylvester, who nickered to her as she tossed him the hay, then climbed into her truck and started it.

"What about Matt?" Grant cried anxiously. "You're not gonna make him walk home, just 'cause he tried—"

"Shut *up*, Grant!"

Just then they heard a thump in the bed of the pickup as Matt swung in. Without looking back to see if he was hanging on, Charlie gunned the motor and turned out of the stockyards in a shower of dust.

Charlie had trouble getting to sleep that night; images and memories of her encounter with Matt played themselves over in her head as she tossed restlessly. Finally she lapsed into a heavy, dream-ridden sleep, in which she and Matt rode Sylvester double into a dressage ring, only to remember just as the audience began to boo that they'd forgotten their top-hats . . .

CHAPTER 4

Horse Sense and Hard Lessons

The next morning Charlie stopped by Sylvester's pen briefly to check that he'd been given water. When he saw her, the gelding's ears came forward and he nickered softly. "I'll be back tonight, Sylvester," she whispered. "Meanwhile, take it easy."

She discovered that Red had successfully managed to stay aboard the gelding, but that the horse had eventually "quit," refusing to buck anymore, but also refusing to do anything else. Foster found later that the horse had cut himself slightly on the left foreleg, and ordered Red to stay off him until it healed.

So Sylvester remained in his solitary pen for the next five days. Charlie made good use of the time, driving over every night after Foster had gone home, to check the animal's water and give him some grain. The higher protein food would give him more energy than just hay. After the second night, Sylvester was waiting by the gate for her when she drove in.

She spent several minutes stroking his shoulder and neck as he munched, talking softly to him. "I wish I could get you cleaned up some," she told him, "feed you more, but somebody might notice. I've gotta figure out some way to get Mr. Foster to let me train you."

On her fourth visit, Charlie tried resting her weight across his back. The first time the gelding put his ears back, swishing his tail warningly, but was too engrossed with his grain to protest further. The second time, he barely looked up. "I'm lucky you're such a chow hound," she said, when he'd finished with the feed. "Here, do you like carrots?"

It was obvious that Sylvester recognized the *snap* of a carrot being broken. He nosed Charlie impatiently, taking the treat with a swift, delicate movement of his long upper lip, crunching down on it with obvious enjoyment. "What a pig," she mumbled, rubbing his jaw. "Here, want another?"

He did; as he chewed, Charlie checked her watch. "Oh, no! Ten till ten—I've been gone nearly an hour and a half. I've got to get home, Sylvester. See you tomorrow."

She drove along the highway at the best speed she dared, fighting the heaviness in her eyelids, once slapping her cheeks stingingly to keep herself alert. The divided white line in the center of the road blurred into a continuous luminous strip as the ancient vehicle swooped over the gentle foothills and into sloping valleys. By the time she reached home, Charlie was almost too tired to undress—and that night, she *didn't* bother with her teeth.

The alarm had been ringing for ten minutes the next morning when Grant finally shook her awake. "Charlie, come on! Wake up! You're gonna be late!"

She roared into the stockyards nearly a half-hour overdue, to find all the yard hands assembled around the breaking pen. As Charlie hopped out of the truck, she spotted Peter, the stableboy, and called, "What's going on, Pete?"

"Tommy John's taking bets on whether Red can ride the big gray this morning."

Oh, no! she thought as she ran over to the fence. Sylvester was inside, blindfolded, a rope twitch gripping his sensitive upper lip in a tight loop of pain, one hind foot tied up underneath his barrel. John Foster threw a worn saddle over the blanket on his back, then reached down to draw up the cinch just as the horse tried to hop sideways, then nearly fell.

"Stand up there!" Red yelled, smacking him with the reins.

Sylvester whipped his head around, blindfold and all, his teeth snapping. Red stepped back hastily out of the way, raising the braided leather reins for another blow. Foster's hand caught his arm. "Cut that out, Red. You're here to ride him, not bully him."

Adams made a face behind the stockyard owner's back, but remained silent. Charlie climbed onto the top rail of the pen, her heart slamming against her ribs, feeling tears threaten behind her eyelids as she saw the horse trembling. *That's not the way with this horse, Mr. Foster!* she wanted to cry out, but forced herself to remain silent. If Red knew that hurting Sylvester would hurt her, the big gray would be in twice as much trouble with the redheaded wrangler.

She watched, her fingers digging hard into the splintered rails of the high-walled breaking pen, biting her lip. Red, moving with his usual catlike grace, put his foot into the stirrup and eased his right leg over the horse's humped back. Foster waited until the wrangler had grasped the reins, then, moving with precise, economical ease, released the rope tying up the hind leg, unwound the twitch, then drew off the blindfold.

Sylvester stood motionless, crouched, as Foster backed slowly away. Red shook the reins and clucked to him, then the little pen seemed to be filled with dust and motion as the gray gelding exploded. Rearing straight up, the horse plunged his head between his knees on the way down, then twisted his body sideways in that high, wrenching rear kick-up wranglers call a "sunfish." Bawling like a maddened bull, he bucked furiously for another two or three leaps, then the yard hands scattered like birds off a wire as he slammed into the fence where they had been sitting. Red yelped as his knee mashed into the heavy rails.

One more wicked sunfish, and Red arced across the pen, to land heavily in the dust.

Sylvester stood in the middle of the pen, snorting loudly, his eyes and nostrils wide. Foster went over to Adams, helped him sit up, then put an arm around the wrangler's shoulders as he climbed swaying to his feet. They went out the gate, leaving the gelding alone in the pen.

"Sylvester," Charlie said, quietly, as she slipped down from the fence. "Come on, boy, it's me."

She began walking steadily toward the gray, murmuring gently, digging a few grains of sweet feed out of her pocket. Sylvester's ears went up, then, as the yard hands voiced their astonishment, he took a step toward her, another, then he was in front of Charlie. His twitching muzzle found and lipped up the sticky feed off her flattened palm, then, with a sigh, he stood quietly. Still talking softly to him, Charlie picked up his reins and led him docilely across the corral.

As she reached the gate, she met Red's amazed stare, then she looked over at John Foster. The old man was furious at being proved wrong, Charlie could tell from his expression, but there was something else in his eyes that made her fight not to grin with delight: respect. For the moment, Sylvester was hers to train, she knew it without asking.

"Come on, Sylvester," she said quietly, and led the horse out of the pen.

"How's Red?" she asked Foster later, as he leaned over the gate to the pen where she was brushing Sylvester.

"He'll be all right. I gave him the rest of the day off." The old man answered, studying the gelding. "I guess you feel pretty smart, putting one over on me like that."

Charlie tried to look innocent as she scrubbed the curry-comb in a circular motion on the horse's mud-and-manure crusted belly. "I just figure that he's one of those horses who likes women but hates men. Wouldn't be the first time we've seen one like that."

"Oh, I agree," said Foster with studied mildness. "But you've been making up to him on the sly, haven't you?"

"Well . . ." She shrugged, trying not to grin. "I gave him water when Red forgot. And one thing led to another . . ."

"Been on him, yet?"

"No. I leaned across his back twice, and he didn't mind too much. I think maybe I ought to try him bareback at first, since he associates saddles with bucking, by now."

Foster nodded, knowing as well as Charlie did that

horses develop connections between items of equipment and what is expected of them. ''Just be sure you're ready to jump clear at the first sign of trouble,'' he said. His sharp blue eyes studied the gray gelding. ''He sure is an ugly sonofagun,'' he murmured. ''I must be crazy to let you spend this much time on one homely bronc.''

''But there's something about this horse,'' Charlie said seriously. ''I don't know why, but I just feel like he could be a winner.''

''At what? He's too big for cutting or roping. Too long-backed to turn on a dime like a good stock horse has to be able to do. Too ugly for pleasure showing or trail classes.''

''I know,'' Charlie agreed. ''But he's got guts, and he uses himself well. Lots of balance and agility, in spite of his size.''

''Might make someone a competitive endurance horse, then,'' Foster said, rubbing thoughtfully at his chin. ''They don't care *what* they look like, as long as they can cover those twenty, forty, or fifty miles in the fastest time, while staying in the best shape.''

''Yeah, maybe that's it. I'll try him up on the butte when I get to that stage.''

''Don't you go messing with him by yourself, at first,'' Foster admonished. ''And don't forget you've got other work to do.''

''I know,'' she said. ''I figured on getting up earlier in the morning to spend extra time with him before work.''

''I swear, Charlie, I've known you since before you needed a bra, and I've never seen you go so hog-wild over anything we've had in here. Even Appy.''

Charlie shrugged. ''I just have this feeling that Sylvester

is special. Aren't you, you homely cuss?'' She rubbed the gelding's neck.

''How old is he?'' Foster asked.

''Haven't looked yet,'' Charlie said, stroking the horse's crest, then continuing down his face to his muzzle. ''Open up here, Sylvester,'' she said, gently inserting a finger in the side of his mouth. ''Let me look at your teeth.''

She pried the gray's jaws apart, examining the centers of his incisors, then peered at the angle of the teeth as they met in the front of the mouth. Sylvester rolled his eyes, but didn't protest further. ''He's got some cups left, and just the beginnings of one set of dental stars,'' she reported, referring to the dark markings in the center of each tooth. ''And his teeth don't angle outward much. I'd say maybe seven or eight.''

''Good. He's young enough. Now if he'll only take to riding.''

''Yeah.''

''When are you gonna try?''

Charlie gathered up the halter rope. ''Now's as good a time as any, I guess.''

''Not without a bridle, Charlie!'' Foster protested, but he was too late. Charlie leaned across the gray's back, letting her arms slide over to his right side. When he showed no response, she grabbed his raggedy mane and, with a quick spring, leaped upward, hooking her elbow over the long gray back, swinging her right leg across, then sitting quickly upright.

Sylvester shied nervously, his eyes rolling. ''Steady, easy, Sylvester,'' Charlie patted him. ''It's me, remember?''

The gray snorted, turning his head to look back at her, as if to verify that she was telling the truth. He sniffed at her leg as it hung down his left side, then stretched his head down. With a slight tug on the halter rope, she brought his nose up. "All right, all right," she soothed, watching the black-tipped ears alertly. They swiveled back and forth, indicating uncertainty on the horse's part, but did not flatten in anger. Cautiously, Charlie shifted her weight on the gray's back, allowing him to feel her legs as they hung down his sides.

Sylvester wasn't happy, tossing his head nervously, reaching out to paw with a forefoot. But he did not buck. "Okay," Charlie breathed. "That was fine for a first time." Nimbly, she swung off, then gave the gray a carrot from her back pocket.

Foster was staring at her again. "You just wake up this morning and decide today was my day to feel foolish, Charlie? Or did you slip him some Ace in that grain?"

Charlie looked faintly scornful at the suggestion that she'd tranquilized the gray gelding. "Neither. I found out a couple of days ago that this horse was broke to ride at some point. There's an old scar from a girth gall on his belly. He must've been sold by whoever broke him and his new owners couldn't handle him."

Foster nodded, tugging thoughtfully at his moustache. "It's happened before," he said. "Spirited animal gets sold to somebody that doesn't know one end from the other, and first thing you know, the horse has lost respect for people, 'cause he knows they can't or won't make him obey. So he picked up more and more bad habits—including bucking, which is how he wound up on the rodeo string."

"Poor guy." Charlie rubbed the gelding's head. "I'd give a lot to know who first trained you, and why she had to let you go."

* * *

Charlie spent nearly five minutes sitting on Sylvester the next day, and determined to try an actual ride the following day. Rummaging through Foster's old storage of unused harness, bridles, and dried-up saddlery produced a *bosal,* a braided rawhide noseband with a heavy knot that would rest beneath the horse's chin. After rigging it with reins and a headstall, she slipped it over Sylvester's head, not wanting to use a bit until his mouth was completely healed of the damage Red's vicious spade had inflicted.

John Foster was on hand, watching from outside the corral as Charlie hopped up, settled herself, then squeezed the gray gently with her legs. "C'mon, Sylvester," she said. "Walk."

The horse trembled, and she could feel the muscles in his back tense. "Careful, he's got a hump in his back," Foster called. "Be ready to bail out."

"C'mon, just walk . . ." Gently, she clucked at the gelding, then he took a hesitant step forward. "That's it. C'mon . . ."

Halfway around the pen, the horse's back began to relax, his ears came forward, and Charlie grinned ecstatically. "All right. That's great, Sylvester!" She patted him, and they continued their slow path around the pen.

After that initial ride, Sylvester's progress was more rapid. Within ten days, Charlie was able to saddle and bridle him, and began using him in her work around the stockyards. The gray never seemed to tire, moving with long, effortless strides through the hottest afternoon's work. It was obvious that he'd never worked cattle, so Charlie began introducing him to them gradually.

But her favorite times with Sylvester came in the early

mornings, when she rode out to check the stock and fences. With tinges of red still staining the sky behind the green-softened buttes, she let the big gray's long strides lengthen to a ground-eating trot, then to a hand-gallop, standing in her stirrups to put her weight forward, over the shoulders, where the horse could carry it better. They created their own wind, storming up the mesa trails, and Charlie, balanced as lightly as a burr over Sylvester's mane, let all her problems slip away with that wind, leaving them far behind, if only for those few minutes.

Often, when she'd pull him to a stop, she'd twist in her saddle to gaze around, still breathing hard from the exertion, letting her heart wind down and take on the peace of the surrounding country. Set as it was in the most mountainous country of Texas, Marfa experienced more rainfall, and the landscape was green, rather than gray-brown. Even the sage and scrubby juniper took on a verdant cast here, away from the desert.

Charlie would sit blinking at the majesty of the rolling foothills and massive, rock-crowned buttes, watching hawks circle lazily against the sky where it deepened overhead to a dark, dark blue. From her high vantage point her eyes could follow their swoop over the valleys dotted with small lakes, toward the nearby Davis Mountains hovering in majestic haze to the north, and something would try to twist its way out of her chest and take wing. She wanted to embrace the land, gather it all up and store it inside her against the hurts and disappointments, the money worries, Red's "pranks," and her late-night thoughts of Matt Grey. Sometimes Charlie, who could not remember crying since her parents' funeral, would find herself battling tears—and not know why.

During those long, solitary rides checking the fences, she began teaching the gray horse the rudiments of dressage, the way she'd seen it illustrated in issues of *Practical Horseman* and *The Complete Training of Horse and Rider* by Colonel Alois Podhajsky. Charlie had found the battered old hardback on Foster's shelves, and spent her lunch hours poring over terms like "collection," "extension," "on the bit," "suppling exercise," and "half-halt," plus many others that seemed almost part of another language.

By studying the illustrations and reading and re-reading the descriptions of movements, she began teaching Sylvester to accept "contact" with the bit. Sylvester was used to being neck-reined and carrying his head straight out in front of him, with little or no pressure on the bit except when Charlie tugged on both reins to signal, "whoa."

To begin lessons in "contact," Charlie fitted the gray with a snaffle bit: a jointed bit that was much gentler on his mouth than the Western bits used by the wranglers. Sylvester mouthed the strange, thick bit skeptically at first, but soon became accustomed to it. During their walks along the fencelines, Charlie began, very gently at first, to take up the reins until they ran in a straight line from the bit to her hands, leaving no slack.

By the end of a week, Sylvester accepted being direct-reined and this mildest version of contact. Slowly, patiently, Charlie began teaching the big gray to bring in his head, bending at his poll (the spot just behind the horse's ears), and to flex his neck muscles. She would sit deep in the saddle, pushing the horse forward by squeezing with her legs and seat, and gently take up on the reins until she could feel his mouth through the bit, alive, waiting for her commands.

It was tedious, absorbing work, and Charlie could spend only a few minutes at a time, at first, because Sylvester's muscles would tire quickly from being exercised in this new fashion. Gradually, the work paid off and the gelding began moving with more balanced, springy gaits. His hindquarters grew stronger, so his movements became smoother and more powerful. The horse also began to fill out from the daily exercise, the better feed, and regular worming every six weeks. His coat took on a healthy sleekness due to daily brushing and improved health, and, though he'd never be a beauty, his looks improved until he was barely recognizable as the bronc who'd arrived at the stockyards that hot summer day.

As autumn approached, Charlie began asking the horse to flex his body more. She practiced making him "bend" his body while riding him in small and large circles, so that, instead of carrying himself stiffly throughout his turns, Sylvester actually curved his spine slightly to match the path of the circle.

Charlie would have been hard put to say exactly *why* she was spending so much time training the horse. While dressage training—like any regular suppling and balance exercises—would prove useful to him as a stock horse or competitive endurance horse, by now she'd taken the gray past the most elementary phases. Charlie was now beginning harder exercises, that were designed to make Sylvester responsive to the slightest signals of her hands, legs, and body.

Part of the reason was the horse himself. Sylvester, once she'd won his trust, proved a willing, honest animal, seldom requiring discipline, but accepting it if he knew that he'd earned it. Charlie carried a long dressage whip beneath the gullet of her saddle, but a harsh word was usually enough to correct the gelding. The whip was used mostly as an adjunct to her leg, providing a little extra prompting when necessary. He genuinely liked and respected Charlie, and, as his condition improved, enjoyed going out for rides. It was obvious to the young woman that the gray gelding had more than his share of "heart" and "bottom"—horseman's terms for courage and determination.

Part of the reason also lay in her wish to expand her own horizons in training horses. Charlie knew that she'd done an excellent job training Appy and several other horses Foster had acquired to be good, "finished" cow ponies. Now she wanted to stretch her abilities a little, try something new. And dressage was the most challenging area of horse training and riding she'd ever encountered. People spent literally a lifetime learning to do it well.

Charlie had two other reasons for working so hard with Sylvester: Red Adams and Matt Grey.

The more time she spent with the gray gelding, the less time she had to work with Adams. In the months since Foster's warning, the redhead had never openly moved against her, but he seldom overlooked a chance to bollix her work or play cruel jokes. On several occasions, Charlie had discovered her lunchtime sandwich half-eaten, and salt in her iced tea. Once she was tripped by an outthrust boot while carrying a heavy bale of hay.

A few weeks later, she discovered just before mounting Appy to herd some calves that the leather cinch strap on her saddle was nearly gnawed through, as though by rats. But Charlie *knew* that rats couldn't have chewed through that much of the tough rawhide in the two hours since she'd taken the saddle off Sylvester. And Red had heard Foster tell her to move the calves. Herding the young Herefords could prove a hard-riding, fast-stopping job, on an experienced cow pony like Appy. If the latigo strap had broken . . .

Charlie began carrying her tack home each night, and double-checking it each time she used it.

Worst of all, one time she'd stopped by to give Sylvester a final check before going home, only to find that a board filled with rusty nails had been shoved under the fence of his pen, near the water trough, where the gray would surely have stepped on it sooner or later. Charlie dragged the length of wood out, then, sweating lest Sylvester should have punctured his foot and gone lame from an abscess, had patiently scrutinized all four feet with a flashlight. Fortunately, the gray was sound.

Charlie's nerves, already strained from the responsibility of supporting her brothers, as well as playing both father and mother to them, began to fray. She considered going to Foster with her accusations, but she remembered the old man's warning words: "Any more fighting or dirty tricks and you're *both* fired. Life's too short." She needed her job too badly to chance losing it. And what would happen to Sylvester without her?

If the shadow of Red Adams loomed over her work days, thoughts of Matt Grey haunted her free time. Every week when she stopped for gas he was there, talking to her, asking her if he could take Grant fishing or riding in his battered jeep. He invited her over to see movies on his VCR on Saturday night. Charlie steadfastly refused any invitations that would require her to be alone with him, telling him laughingly that she didn't trust him any further than she could throw Sylvester.

But if she stopped to examine her own motives in refusing to spend time with Matt, she had to admit that the real person she didn't trust was . . . herself. Deep inside her, she knew that Matt was somebody who might be able to touch her, might be able to get past her defenses to find that lonely, needing person that she only encountered when she woke late at night, and couldn't go back to sleep . . .

"Why do you keep asking?" she flared one evening when she ran into him at the Safeway and he insisted on carrying her groceries out to her pickup. "You know I'm going to say no, Matt."

"No to a dinner in Alpine? Tomorrow's Sunday. You can drop Grant and Seth off at my house and my mom will watch 'em. C'mon, Charlie. You've been doing nothing but work with that gray horse for *weeks.*" Matt stood waiting quietly for her answer, but there was a restrained eagerness in his features, his lean, muscular body, that told her how much he wanted to be with her.

Charlie shook her head, backing away half a step. "I'm sorry, Matt. I can't. School's back in session, and I have to check the boys' homework—"

"Not 'can't'—*won't.*" Something flickered deep in his dark eyes that might have been anger. "Charlie, every time I ask you, you're busy. If you're worried about what happened in the barn that night, if you want I'll promise not to touch you. But don't give me the cold shoulder."

Charlie shook her head helplessly. "Matt, I'm just not ready to let myself get involved with anyone but Seth and Grant—and Sylvester. But that's because none of them threaten me like you do. I feel like you'd be happy if you could swallow me up. Why do you keep asking me? I hate telling you 'no.' "

He sighed, kicking at a rock on the parking lot with the worn toe of his Tony Lamas. "I'll be switched if I know myself, Charlie. I ought to have my head examined for hanging around, just waiting to get put down again. There's plenty of other girls would go out with me, you know," he grinned ruefully, "girls who can't match you for orneriness by a mile."

Charlie settled the last of her groceries into the cab of the pickup and took out her keys. "Really? That ornery, huh?"

"Yeah. But somehow, when I'm with 'em I have trouble staying awake. All they want to talk about are who's dating who and who's driving what, and who's pregnant and by who. At least you're never boring. Cussed, but not boring."

She pushed her hair out of her eyes, chuckling as she turned to hop up into the Ford. "I've got to get on home."

"Charlie . . ." he put his hand on her arm, his fingers long and strong against her tanned skin. She turned back, trying to ignore the sudden jump of her heart.

"What?"

"If you won't go to Alpine, can we go riding tomorrow? Foster'd let you borrow a horse for me. He knows I can handle one."

Charlie began to laugh, helplessly. "What is this, 'if you can't beat 'em, join 'em'?"

He shrugged. "Something like that. We could take a picnic in my old saddlebags."

She gave in suddenly and nodded. "All right. *If* your mom will watch the boys. You can ride Appy."

CHAPTER 5

On the Range

Matt adjusted the stirrups on his worn old Bona Allen saddle. "Been so long since I've been on a horse that I've gotten taller," he mumbled.

"Here, do you mind tying this on your saddle?" Charlie asked, extending the saddlebags. "I'm riding English today, and my saddle doesn't have ties."

Matt fastened the leather pouches in place, checked his girth by sliding his hand underneath Appy's belly, then, finding that the little horse had "blown up" or held his breath while the cinch was fastened, tightened the latigo so the saddle wouldn't slip. He mounted, checking his stirrups. "Hey, Charlie, I'm ready."

"So am I," she said, leading Sylvester out of the barn. Matt stared at the big gray in surprise. The horse was sleek and well-muscled, his black-specked coat slick. He stood quietly as Charlie mounted.

"Boy, he sure looks different than the last time I saw him. Why the English tack?"

"Allows me to keep contact on his mouth, and he can feel my legs better when I signal."

They moved out of the stockyards. Matt spent a minute demonstrating to Appy that, even though it had been several years since he'd ridden, he still remembered how. The little horse quickly abandoned his notion of bucking and shying at every shadow, settling into a comfortable jog.

"Let's take the trail up to the top of the mesa," Charlie called back to him. "It's just the right length for a pleasure ride."

"Fine," Matt called back, watching Sylvester trot out ahead of him. The big gray moved lightly, his strides even and balanced, his hindquarters well "under" his body so he moved like a coiled spring, relaxed, yet ready for commands. He carried his head down, his nose in, holding the bit in his mouth as gently and alertly as a mother cat carrying a kitten. Charlie sat on his back as though her seat were glued to the saddle, only her midsection rocking back and forth slightly in time to the horse's strides.

"Hey!" Matt yelled. "Slow down! You want me to have to run poor Appy all the way up there?"

"I'm sorry," she called back. Her hands tightened almost imperceptibly on the reins, and Sylvester dropped to a walk.

"What kind of trot was that?" Matt asked, as Appy jogged up beside her. Sylvester was several hands taller than the Appaloosa, and their eyes were almost on a level as they rode.

"I'm working on trying an extended trot," she said. "He's collecting nicely, but I need more impulsion."

"Talk English, okay? Remember, I'm just a poor dumb

cowpoke,'' Matt said plaintively, using an exaggerated drawl.

Charlie laughed. ''What I meant is that he's responding well to my hands, keeping good contact with the bit, but that I have to work harder to make him go forward.''

Matt shook his head. ''That's not much better, Charlie.''

She sighed. ''You're right. I've been spending all my spare time reading up on dressage, and I guess I'm starting to sound like a book. Let me see if I can do better . . .'' she continued, explaining the concepts at some length as they rode along

He listened, enjoying the unguarded enthusiasm on her face, the excitement in her voice. She really *did* know a lot about this dressage stuff, he realized. When she finally stopped, he was beginning to understand why it had taken her so long to get this far. But there was something he still didn't comprehend. ''Well, I can tell that he moves differently than Appy,'' he said. ''And I can see how all this balance and flexing and suppling would help him carry himself better. But they don't give prizes for collected or extended gaits out here on the mesa. So why keep at it?''

''I don't know,'' she admitted. ''In the East they have shows, where you can be evaluated and judged on dressage, just like they judge cutting horses out here. If only . . .'' she sighed.

''Well, he sure is pretty to watch,'' Matt said. ''And the way you sort of blend in with him like you're just one critter instead of two, that's pretty, too.'' He grinned at her. ''And you don't just *ride* pretty, Charlie.''

She flushed, not looking at him. ''Let's lope.''

Matt touched Appy with his heels lightly and the little horse sprang into a rocking-chair canter as they took the last gentle slope up to the top of the mesa. Sylvester snorted as Charlie gave him more rein, then, effortlessly, his strides lengthened until he was far ahead of them. The gray gelding's long legs covered ground like pistons, tirelessly. Even Appy was breathing hard by the time Charlie drew rein and they caught up.

"He's in some kind of shape!" she exulted, her eyes sparkling from wind-whipped tears, her short brown hair standing straight up. "It's like being on top of a thunderbolt!"

"Maybe," Matt caught his breath with an effort, "maybe you ought to take him to the racetrack and forget this dressage stuff."

"Oh, he's not fast enough for that," she said, as they began walking the horses slowly along the top of the mesa. "But over a distance he could do in most of the horses I've ever been on. He never seems to get tired."

"Might make an endurance horse."

"That's what Mr. Foster thinks."

"Well, what do you think?"

"I think," she tugged absently at a lock of the gelding's mane in front of her pommel, "that I'm gonna hate to see him sold, more than any other horse I've ever worked with."

A scheme began forming at the back of Matt's mind. "How much do you think Foster'd want for him?"

Charlie shook her head. "I don't know how much he's got in him, but I know some of those endurance horses can cost a thousand or more."

Matt sighed. He didn't have that kind of money to spare. "Where do you want to eat lunch?"

"How about here?"

They dismounted, removing the horses' bridles and tying

them by their halters and lead ropes to the short, scrubby juniper trees. Charlie dug sandwiches and a canteen out of the saddlebags. "Peanut butter and honey," she said. "I didn't have anything else in the house."

"Look in the other bag," he directed. "I brought some hard-boiled eggs and carrot sticks."

They shared the food in companionable silence, passing the canteen back and forth. The horses dozed in the bright autumn noontime sun. "I like picnics this time of the year," Matt said. "No bugs."

"Yeah."

Matt munched thoughtfully on a carrot stick, then swallowed. "You've got a birthday coming up in a couple of weeks."

She looked at him. "Yeah. So?"

"Anything special you want?"

Charlie laughed humorlessly. "Yeah. One of those ray guns that'll disintegrate things without leaving any traces."

"For who? Me?"

"No," she gave him a sideways glance, shaking her head. "You, I can deal with. I wanted it for Red."

"What's he doing besides being a pimple on the backside of the planet?"

"You pretty much said it right there." She made a face. "I don't know how anyone who hates animals can want to work with them—but he does."

"That's because pushing around animals makes him feel human," Matt observed. "You could always find another job . . . or let me take care of him for you."

"Don't you go getting all macho on me, Matt. And I don't want another job."

"You figuring on spending your life working with horses? Is that what you want to do?"

She gave him a quick nod, her blue-gray eyes very serious. "Yep. That's what I want to do. I want to train horses."

"You can't make any money at that, even if you could find some to train."

"I could do all right if I had a reputation . . . people would look me up."

"How would you get a reputation?"

"I don't know. Train a famous horse. Work in a big stable for awhile."

"Sounds kind of unlikely to me," he said, then frustration made him amend, "frankly, it sounds impossible, Charlie! What's wrong with just working in some kind of ordinary job, and having a horse of your own? I'd never object to *that*—it's just having you out there, day after day, risking your neck training broncs, that drives me crazy! Grow up and face reality!"

"You just don't understand, Matt Grey!" she turned on him, anger making her cheeks flush. "I *am* grown up. I spend every day being grown up and mature, looking at life the way it is. And it's because I'm that way that I don't trust you, and I'm not letting you tell me what I can do!" She was so angry that she stumbled over her words. "That's all men want, to own you, to make you just a little part of them. The whole thing stinks!"

He stared at her speechlessly. She was shaking as she looked at him. "I watched my mother do it, every day, every week, every year. I watched her turn into a little part of Daddy, until there wasn't anything of Lena left at all. Then, when he'd go out and drink, and mess around, and come home and hit her, she *never* wondered what the heck was wrong with him—she wondered what was wrong with *her*."

Charlie clenched a handful of Saran wrap, pulling at it with her other hand until it stretched into thinness, then ripped. Her voice was so low Matt had to strain to hear her. "I tried to tell her it wasn't her fault, but it was too late. It was like she'd disappeared from the inside out. Nobody's ever gonna make me disappear . . . nobody's ever gonna drown me like that. Never. The only person I'm *guaranteed* to live my life with is *myself,* Matt. You ought to think about that, the next time you find yourself telling me what *you* want *me* to do."

Furiously, she began stuffing the sandwich wrappings back into the saddlebags. Matt finally found his voice. "I didn't—I never knew it was that bad, Charlie. I think . . ." he took a deep breath. "I'll think about what you said. Maybe I *was* leaning on you . . ."

Nearly a minute went by, as she fiddled with the buckle on the saddlebag. "Most guys wouldn't ever admit they might be wrong," she said, finally.

"Well, maybe I'm not most guys."

She nodded, and a faint smile touched her mouth for a second. "Maybe you're not."

Charlie rode Sylvester to work calves in the auction barn the next day. She was thinking about the picnic, about what a nice day it had turned out to be, as she automatically reined Sylvester back and forth after the fat Black Angus calves. The gray gelding was still a little spooky about riding into the dimness of the barn from the brightness of the yard. "Come on, Sylvester," she said, urging him closer to where Red was holding the gate. "Can't let 'em turn back now."

"Get that nag moving!" Red snarled as the gray horse sidled through, snorting, after the calves. "I got work to do!"

Deliberately, he let the gate swing closed on Sylvester's rump. The impact and rattle of the boards of the wooden gate against his buttocks and hocks panicked the gray, causing him to leap frantically forward. Charlie, who was leaning over, getting ready to close the gate, was caught off balance and fell, crashing hard into the gatepost. The horse's feet skidded on the hard-packed clay and he went down on his side with a thump.

Charlie slid dazedly to the ground, her wind knocked out, white sparks dancing before her eyes. She heard Red curse, then realized that the gelding was climbing to his feet. Trying to call his name, she managed only a hiss of pain. Then came the rapid thump of hoofbeats, and Charlie, with an effort that left her shaking, pulled herself up. "Sylvester!" she managed to croak.

Too late. Even as she watched, the horse began to gallop, cleaving a path through the frightened bawling calves like a knife. He reached the fence at the end of the aisle at a dead run, and didn't even slow down. As elegantly as if he'd done it every day of his life, Sylvester gathered himself, launched, then floated over the five-foot-nine-inch fence as though it were a clump of sagebrush.

As Charlie watched in horror he landed, then picked up more speed, vanishing into the distance—in the direction of the highway.

CHAPTER 6

Runaway Bad Luck

''Get him!'' Red shouted, turning and running toward his Kawasaki. Charlie whirled, saw Appy standing in the pen, dozing, and snatched up his bridle as she ran by the tackroom.

''Appy!'' she called, trying to keep the fear out of her voice as she walked toward him. She didn't want to spook him, or she'd never catch him.

''Good boy!'' Quickly Charlie tossed the reins around the stock pony's neck, then tugged the headstall over his ears. Scrambling up bareback, she reined the Appaloosa hard out the gate in the direction Sylvester had taken, slapping him on the neck with the reins. ''Get up, Appy!''

Appy leaped forward with the spring of a frightened deer, flattening out as he raced toward the highway. Even as they tore along the dirt road, Charlie could hear horns begin to honk up ahead. Straining her eyes, she saw Sylvester clear the wire fence that separated the pasture from the blacktop. "Oh, no!" she mumbled, urging Appy to his fastest run, bending low over his mane.

Sylvester reached the highway just as a massive semi thundered by and let loose a deafening blast on its air horn. The gray reared wildly, his eyes bulging in panic, then turned and began racing parallel to the road. Charlie reined Appy after him, seeing Red cutting across the field ahead of them on his bike, obviously hoping to get far enough in front of the runaway horse to turn him back.

She clung desperately to Appy's back, one hand wrapped in his mane. The cowpony dug in harder, racing after Sylvester. Charlie's patient training had paid off—once he realized his rider wanted him to head off the riderless horse in front of him, Appy needed little guidance. Ears flat to his head, the little Appaloosa was now gaining on the frightened, confused Sylvester.

All along the highway, cars slowed, honking, as men, women and children hung out of their windows, yelling and laughing as they pointed at the gray gelding. Charlie, leaning over Appy's neck as he seemed to gain on the other horse by inches, experienced a terrible slow-motion sense of unreality: she had trouble convincing herself the whole dreadful thing was actually *happening*.

Ahead of them, Red blasted up the embankment on his motorcycle, opening the throttle full out, waving at Sylvester in an attempt to turn him away from the highway. But instead, seeing the roaring vehicle appear suddenly in front of him frightened the gray horse out of what little sense of self-preservation he still had. He spun hard on his hindquarters, bolting out into the middle of the highway.

"No!" Charlie cried in horror as tires screeched. Vehicles piled into each other like dominoes, the *wham!* of crashing metal mingling hideously with the sound of broken windshields and human screams. She spotted a gray hide in the midst of the melee, and turned Appy across the road as she saw Sylvester, miraculously untouched, reach the opposite side of the highway. A pickup truck pulling a flatbed was slewed across his path, but the horse soared over it with room to spare.

Charlie squeezed Appy with her left leg and the little horse responded instantly, ducking left, circling the truck to come up alongside Sylvester. "Whoa, Sylvester!" she shouted.

As Appy moved closer, herding the gray away from the road, she reached out, grabbing his remaining rein—the other dangled broken from his bit—and pulled him to a stop.

Sitting atop the blowing Appaloosa beside the exhausted, quivering Sylvester, Charlie turned to look back at the highway and groaned aloud. Traffic was stopped for nearly a mile.

Charlie looked out the fly-specked window of Foster's office, seeing the last of the tow trucks and police cars turn and pull away on the distant highway. The stockyards owner's voice rose to a shout behind her: ". . . and it looks like Mrs. Preston's suffered a broken arm! Now *she'll* sue, too, you can bet your idiot rear on that, Adams! I oughta turn around and sue your parents, that's what I oughta—"

"But it wasn't *my* fault, Mr. Foster!" The lanky redhead had lost his bravado for once. Charlie watched as he took a hasty step backward in the face of Foster's rage.

"Any horse with a brain in his head woulda stopped at the fence—one of those fences! You realize how *high*—"

"Not when the horse was as scared as Sylvester was after you spooked him," Charlie cut in, eyeing Adams with hatred she made no attempt to mask. "You did it on purpose, you lousy—"

"That's enough, Charlie," Foster snapped. "It doesn't do any good to go over it again. What I'm looking at here is four lawsuits I already know about, plus the Lord only knows how many will turn up in the next couple of days. My insurance company will probably drop me, the mayor's on my back, even the SPCA—!!" He stopped, controlling himself with a visible effort. "That's it, Adams. You're through."

"You can't fire me!" the wrangler flared, giving Charlie a venomous look. "I got—"

"You got nothing more to say. You had your chance here, Red. I'll write you a letter. You can probably get a job on the track in El Paso."

"Fire *her!*" Red shouted, pointing at Charlie. "I can break six horses in the time it takes her to break one. I'll do her work and mine too. *And* Peter's. Fire Peter, too. I'll do it all . . . me and Tommy John. Please!"

"Grovel, Red," Charlie was unable to restrain herself. "I don't see you laughing, now that the joke's on *you*."

Red lunged for her, then stopped as Foster stepped between them. The old man looked down at Charlie sorrowfully. "You're through too, honey. I'm sorry."

She looked up at him, her voice an incredulous whisper. "Mr. Foster?"

"I can't help it. I talked to the cops and the mayor. You're underage just like he is. I never shoulda hired you in the first place. I've broken the law, not getting you work permits, and my insurance probably won't cover you 'cause of that. It's a mess.''

The stuffy little room seemed to spin around her. Charlie reached for her voice, found it somewhere. ''Fired? You mean it?''

''Grovel, Rail. It's so macho.'' The wrangler snickered and Foster gave him a look. Red shut up.

''All right, get out of here. Both of you.'' The stockyards owner turned away, his tall frame slumping wearily.

Adams headed for the door, turning to look back at Charlie. She bristled at him. ''Would you just go!''

He slammed the door, leaving Charlie and Foster alone. The old man sighed, rubbing the back of his neck, not looking at her. ''I can't keep you, Charlie. I wish I could, but it's impossible.''

She began to shake with the effort not to cry. ''I don't want to wait tables. I don't want to run a cash register at the Safeway. I want to break and train horses.''

''I'm sorry.'' He still wouldn't look at her.

''Want to see me grovel, Mr. Foster?''

''Not a whole lot,'' he said, finally looking at her. ''But even if you did, it wouldn't change my mind.''

''What about Sylvester?'' she asked around the tightness in her aching throat.

''He's broke. I'll sell him for a trail and pleasure horse. To someone who'll be decent to him.''

Charlie nodded, barely holding herself together, and walked out of the office. She closed the door quietly behind her, her stubby nails scraping the metal knob with a tiny, final sound.

CHAPTER 7

Trapped in a Nightmare

Charlie hefted her saddle across her back and, stooping carefully to avoid dropping the bridle slung over her shoulder, picked up her worn canvas duffle bag. Straightening, she took a last look around the tackroom at the stockyards, smelling the warm smells of oiled leather, feed, and horse sweat. Tears threatened again, but she bit her lip fiercely, willing them back. She couldn't go home to the boys with her eyes all red and swollen; that would scare them worse than the news that she'd been fired.

Staggering a little under the load she left the barn, heading for her pickup. The sky was darkening to cobalt except in the west, where the sun had just set in a flaming splash of gold and crimson.

Red was sitting on his Kawasaki, watching her approach, drinking a Bud. Charlie glared at him as she slung the saddle into the back of the Ford. ''I hope you're satisfied, Red. Maybe *you* can just pick up and head for the track at

El Paso, but some people can't move around as easy as all that."

He tilted the beer back for a last swallow, then tossed it onto the packed dirt of the parking area. Reaching for the carrying case on the back of the motorcycle, he took out another, popped it open and swallowed, his throat rippling. When he lowered the can he grinned wolfishly at her, belched loudly, and shrugged. "Too bad, honey. Them's the breaks."

Charlie realized he was a little drunk, and she didn't like the way he was looking at her. "What happened to your saddle, Red?" she asked, nervously, feeling in her duffle bag for her keyring.

"Sold it to Peter for a hundred bucks."

"But I heard you tell Tommy John that Sylvester had cracked the tree when he slammed it against the fence."

"Yeah, well, I guess I forgot to mention that to the dummy. Teach him to be more careful next time."

Charlie turned away. "Scumbag . . ." She opened the door of the pickup, keys in hand, lifting one leg to step up—

—and something heavy hit her in the back. Arms like bars of iron closed around her waist, pushing her into the cab of her truck. She smelled beer in a rush of hot breath past her ear.

It took her a stunned second to realize that Red had actually attacked her, but recovering, she began twisting wildly, hammering at his forearms with her fists, trying to kick backward. "Get offa me, you pig!"

He laughed, and the stench of his breath made her gag. "You got me fired, you little slut. Now you're gonna pay for that."

His hands came up to grab at the buttons of her shirt. Charlie realized with the worst jab of fear she'd ever known that simply roughing her up wasn't his intention anymore; he was going to try to rape her!

She screamed, clawing at him, so frightened that she was afraid for a second she might wet herself or faint. One hand clamped brutally over her mouth, just as his other succeeded in ripping her shirt down the front.

He thrust her facedown onto the seat of the Ford, then tried to turn her over. She let him, going limp for a moment, hoping to make him think she had fainted—then once he relaxed his grip, she sank her fingers viciously into his face, clawing hard for his eyes. She bit the hand covering her mouth, feeling blood spatter her chin, and managed to jerk out another scream before he slapped her brutally across the face.

She dug her fingers into his cheek, groping again for his eyes, thrashing beneath him, kicking wildly. She was wiry and strong, but he outweighed her by more than sixty pounds. She knew that, sooner or later, she was going to lose.

Her boot heel caught in the steering wheel, and the blast of the Ford's horn filled the still evening air. Charlie kept up the pressure, praying that someone was still in the stockyards to hear.

Red tried to grab her bra, but Charlie jabbed her thumb into his eye and he howled, jerking his head back like a wild-eyed steer. The blare of the horn went on.

He slapped her, hard, across the face, once, twice—three times, and Charlie felt consciousness slipping away from her, dissolving into a grayish-red mist. She struggled to keep fighting, keep up the pressure on the horn . . . dimly, she was aware that Red was fumbling at his belt—

The wrangler's weight was lifted clean off her as though by a crane as he was jerked backwards, out of the truck. Charlie struggled to sit up, in time to see John Foster literally pick up the youth by his collar, flinging him away from the truck. Red rolled over, his jeans slipping down, and he struggled to pull them up as he staggered to his feet. Foster's big-knuckled left connected with the side of his face, followed by a right that broke the redhead's nose with an audible *crack*.

Red sprawled in the dust, staring up at the old man with terror filling his eyes. "Get up," the stockyards owner grated, rubbing his knuckles. "Give me an excuse to kill you."

Adams stayed down, sobbing, spraying blood and mucus from his nose as he whimpered.

Charlie didn't wait to see any more. Pulling her ripped shirt around her, she tied it in a knot at her midriff, then found her keyring on the floor. Panting, shaking, she picked up a handful of tissues, began wiping blood and saliva off her face as she started the Ford.

The door slammed shut from the pickup's momentum as Charlie rammed it into gear, conscious only of the need to get home, to take a shower. She felt as though she'd never be clean again.

CHAPTER 8

Hard Times

The next two months were the most difficult ones Charlie Railsberg had yet experienced. Unable to collect unemployment insurance due to her age and her lack of a valid work permit, she was thrown back on her small savings and the two hundred-dollar monthly check from her father's insurance—a benefit that ran out one month after she'd lost her job.

She found that none of the other local ranches would hire her because of her age and the fact that winter was a slow season for them. The only jobs available to her were those any high school kid might land: bagging groceries, sweeping floors, waiting tables. Charlie tried all three. Her stint as a waitress ended one day when she upended a plate of ham and eggs on the head of a trucker who pinched her, following it up with a cup of ice water into his lap. She swept and cleaned at the Marfa National Bank and at the office of the local weekly newspaper—*The Marfa Indepen-*

dent. But both jobs entailed only about 20 hours a week, and Charlie needed full-time employment.

She managed to land a job as a clerk at the Nu-Way Grocery, but had a frustrating run-in with a computer price scanner, causing shoppers in the Express Line to wait over half an hour to purchase their "Eight Items or Less." Then, when she finally got the automatic equipment to work, it added prices with such enthusiasm that a 24-can case of soda pop suddenly acquired a value of over $168.00 . . .

"Thanks, Roy," Charlie said, taking off her checker's smock and handing it to the manager. "I'd rather break twenty broncs than face twenty more customers. I appreciate your giving me the chance, though."

She left the market, seeing that there was still daylight left, and after a second's hesitation, turned her truck in the opposite direction from home.

The stockyards were closed for the day; the wranglers had gone home. Charlie parked the Ford in her old spot in the parking area, and sat looking out, unable to repress a shudder. It had been three weeks since she'd been there, and she'd heard through the grapevine that Red had lighted out for Mexico the same night that John Foster had brought him home to his parents, bleeding and beaten, and told them that if their son ever showed his face around town again, he'd swear out a warrant for his arrest.

After a moment, she squared her shoulders. Red Adams was gone, and she *had* to know how Sylvester was doing.

Charlie got out of the pickup and walked around the barn to his pen, her footsteps echoing on the beaten earth. Before she rounded the corner there was the drum of trotting hooves, and the horse's nicker. She broke into a run. ''Sylvester!''

The big gray pawed excitedly at seeing her, rumbling again. ''Well, how have you been? I missed you.'' Charlie swung up onto the gate and the horse came over and pushed her impatiently with his big bony head. ''Still the same pig as ever,'' she laughed, scratching his jaw. ''You've been fed by now.''

She glanced toward the unlighted office at the top of the auction barn. ''Hey . . .'' she said, slowly, as an idea occurred to her, ''you want to go for a little ride? Mr. Foster probably doesn't have anybody to exercise you . . . you're getting fat, as a matter of fact, Sylvester.''

She hastily found the English saddle and snaffle bridle. The gray gelding was feeling his oats after his vacation, and crowhopped and shied when she first swung up on him, snorting with excess energy. ''You quiet down,'' Charlie said, showing him her dressage whip. ''I don't have time to put up with foolishness.''

Sylvester rolled his eyes, but quieted in the face of Charlie's warning. She worked him for a while in the pen, then opened the gate and took him up to the mesa for a run. On the way back, in the gathering dark after sunset, she practiced collection and extension, delighted to find that Sylvester remembered almost everything he'd been taught.

''I'll be back,'' she whispered, after she'd untacked him and brushed him carefully to remove any saddle marks. ''I'll come whenever I can.''

Sylvester blew gustily, nosing her for carrots.

* * *

In his dark office, John Foster stood by the window, looking down at Charlie's slim form in the twilight as she climbed into her truck and drove away. He shook his head and sighed, scratching thoughtfully at the back of his neck.

After a few more minutes, he went outside and climbed into his truck, then drove into Marfa, parking outside Quanch's Bar. As he entered, he saw Matt Grey sitting at the bar. Steve Hawkins, the bartender, looked up. "Evening, John. What'll it be?"

"Draft." Foster walked over and sat down beside the young man. "Hi, Matt."

"Hi, John. How's business?"

"Same as usual this time of year. Slow. Everyone's buying turkeys, not beef."

"How's the mess over that traffic pileup going?"

"The insurance is going to handle it, but it's bound to raise my rates."

"Tough break, but I guess these things happen sometimes."

"Yeah." Foster sipped at his beer, not bothering to wipe the foam off his moustache.

"Heard Charlie quit the Nu-Way today."

"Yeah? That's about the third job, isn't it?"

"Yeah." Matt drew patterns on the bar with spilled beer, not looking up. "She's just too much of a maverick to take a lot of bull off anybody. You spoiled her, John."

"Guess maybe I did." Foster looked over at him. "But I can't see taking her back . . . for her own good, more than mine. She's gotta learn to do something besides train horses. You can't make a living at that, 'less you're the tops."

"I think Charlie thinks she could be."

"Maybe she could, Matt. She's a good rider. But you need to build a reputation, and you can't do that around here. Not in Southwest Texas."

"What happened to Red Adams, John? He hightailed it out of town like a scared jackrabbit, and I heard somebody busted his nose. You know anything about that?"

"Yeah." Foster rubbed a recent scar across his right knuckles. "He's lucky I didn't kill him. When I fired him, I guess he decided he didn't have anything to lose, so he jumped Charlie out in the parking lot. I barely got there in time. He was serious 'bout it."

Matt jerked upright on his barstool. "You mean he tried—"

"Shhhh." Foster nodded bleakly. "You don't want that getting around. Folks might talk about Charlie, and she never did nothin' to make him think—"

Matt began cursing, quietly, under his breath. "She never told me. I'd have caught that lousy—"

"It's over now, and he didn't do anything but scare her pretty bad. Take it easy, son. I understand Red's folks have put their place up for sale—he doesn't dare come back to this town. I talked to Stan Marsh, the Captain of Police, and he's keeping an eye out just to make sure, but after the licking I gave that little whelp, I'm betting he's *still* running. Sucker's a coward under that smart-talkin' front he put up."

The younger man subsided, but his eyes still glittered angrily. "Why didn't she tell me, John?"

"Maybe she was afraid it'd get back to Grant and Seth. She's having a hard enough time keeping that family together, without a bunch of nasty rumors."

"Yeah." Matt looked over at Foster, concerned. "I

pumped gas today for Mrs. Daniels, the Child Welfare social worker for the county. She was asking me a bunch of nosy questions about how long Charlie had been out of work . . . stuff like that.''

''Uh, oh. You suppose she's thinking about putting those kids in Boys' Camp?''

''I sure hope not. That would *kill* Charlie. She lives for those kids . . . and that horse, Sylvester. You still got him?''

''Yeah, I got him. Somehow I just couldn't get it up to sell him. I rode him myself, the other day, just to see what she'd been doing with him.''

''And?''

''He moves nice. Back East, he might bring quite a piece of change, in spite of his looks. But you never know. That's a pretty chancy business.''

Matt stared glumly into his beer. ''I was thinking 'bout trying to buy him for her, for Christmas. But she can't support a horse with no job, and I know she won't let me help her that much. She's like that . . . ornery.''

Foster smiled wryly. ''Sounds like you got it bad, Matt.'' It was a statement rather than a question and Matt didn't bother to answer; both of them knew the old man was right.

Charlie's money was running out. She paid the second month's rent on the old Schultz out of the last of her ''rainy day'' savings. Grant and Seth spent their afternoons scavenging for old bottles and cans, and they lived off eggs, canned beans, and macaroni and cheese.

Her only respite from the day-to-day struggle to find a job became the time she spent over at the stockyards, just before dark. Sometimes she took Grant and Seth to watch while she rode Sylvester. She began teaching him flying lead changes, where the horse is required to change leads at the canter without dropping to a trot first. She taught the gray to change leads every ten strides, then every five, then every three—his slow, collected canter and the skipping lead changes made him look as if he were performing some kind of graceful equine ballet as he zig-zagged across the ring.

Remembering the way the gelding had cleared the high stockyards fence, Charlie constructed some simple jumps out of cinderblocks and split rails, and began training the horse to jump.

First she taught him to lunge, standing in the center of the ring while he circled around her on a long line, controlling his speed with taps of her long buggy whip against the ground. When Sylvester could lunge easily at the walk, trot, and canter, she tried jumping him on the long line. He cleared the small jump as though it weren't even there, naturally arching his back and picking up his feet.

Charlie was excited. The horse was a born jumper, and the higher she constructed the little obstacle, the more fun he seemed to have clearing it.

She read up on jumping in back issues of *Practical Horseman,* studying riding positions intently, seeing the way one bent low over the horse's neck, allowing the reins to follow the motion of the animal's head so they never jerked the bit.

Charlie began practicing jumping, both in the ring and out on the mesa, over gullies and clumps of brush. As an expert rider, she found keeping her balance over obstacles far easier than maintaining the delicate, pinpoint control and concentration required by the dressage exercises. In only a few weeks, Sylvester was successfully clearing the cinderblock jump at three-foot-six, from either a trot or canter. Jumping the big horse was like flying, as he gathered himself, pushed off with his powerful hindquarters, and soared over obstacles.

Charlie knew that sooner or later John Foster was bound to get wind of what she was doing with his horse, but she didn't think about it. She *had* to ride; days that she couldn't get over to the stockyards to see Sylvester were days when her problems seemed so overwhelming that a couple of times she found herself wishing she could just run away from her responsibilities and never look back.

One evening she was working Sylvester on flying changes of lead when John Foster rode into the stockyards on his chestnut mare, Penny, and saw her. He dismounted, letting Penny stand ground-tied, her reins hanging, and walked over to the ring. Charlie could tell from his strides that he was angry. "All right, Charlie, this has gone far enough. What do you think you're doing with my horse?"

"Teaching him flying changes, Mr. Foster. Want to see?" She cantered Sylvester toward him. "Pretty good, huh?"

"What about your job at MacDonald's?"

"I got fired. Watch." She turned Sylvester toward the jump and he soared over it. He turned and came back across the ring at an extended trot, his forefeet flashing in long, balanced strides, then, when Charlie sat back in her saddle and tightened her fingers, obediently stopped with all four feet squarely beneath him. "Pretty good, huh? I told you he was special."

"Why'd you get fired *this* time?"

"Some guy drove up to the drive-in window and ordered a danish and coffee to go—at three o'clock this afternoon. I told him we didn't have danish after ten o'clock in the morning. He told me to make it one apple-raisin danish and one cheese danish. I told him we didn't have 'em, and he cussed me out. So I returned the favor. End of story." She glared at Foster defiantly.

"Charlie . . ." the old man sighed.

"But never mind about that, Mr. Foster. I've been thinking about Sylvester. They've got articles in *Practical Horseman* about horses that are good at endurance, jumping, and dressage. They call 'em Eventing horses, and they show them in Three-Day Events. Like in the Olympics. We could show him in one of those Eventing shows, and then sell him to the Olympic team. I'll bet they'd pay—"

"What are you doing for a job?" he interrupted, glaring at her.

She fiddled with Sylvester's white mane. "I'll find something. Honest, Mr. Foster, he can jump a house! I saw him jump a pickup truck once, that day he got away. I don't want to hurt him bringing him along too fast, but he loves it. Never tries to run out, or refuses—I *know* he'd make a great Event horse. He could go to the Olympics—"

"Charlie!"

She took a deep breath and finally looked at him.

"You're not to ride him anymore," Foster said, heavily.

"Even after work?"

"Nobody gets fired from McDonald's, Charlie. Not if they're willing to work. Not unless they have an attitude problem. You're gonna have to get over yours, honey, if you're going to continue taking care of those brothers of yours." He looked over at Seth, who was sitting in the cab of the pickup, coloring.

Charlie bit her lip. "All right, Mr. Foster."

She pulled away from the stockyards a few minutes later, not letting herself believe that Foster really meant what he had said. He *couldn't* take Sylvester away from her. Inwardly she knew the old man was fond of her, and that he wanted the best for her. All right then, she decided, she'd get another job and stick with it. If she was working, he couldn't have any objection to her riding the gray.

She was supposed to pick up Grant from Webb's, where he'd been spending the day doing odd jobs for Matt. Looking down at her gas gauge, she noted without surprise that it was steady on the "E" mark.

When she reached the gas station, she honked as she pulled up in front of the pumps. Grant tore out from the auto repair bay, yelling excitedly, swinging something limp and bloody. He raced up to the pickup's window, and jumped in beside Seth. He was carrying two skinned and gutted rabbits. "Lookit this, Charlie! We'll have meat tonight! I shot 'em myself, plus three more. I gave them to Matt for his mom to fix for dinner, 'cause it was his gun and ammunition, and besides, he taught me how to shoot."

Charlie grinned at him. "I'm so proud of you! Did Matt skin them for you?"

"Nope," Grant said proudly, "I did it myself."

A profound "Yuucchh" was Seth's comment.

Matt Grey came out of the service bay, wiping his hands on a rag. "Hi, Charlie. See what Grant got?"

"Yeah, I was just telling him I was proud of him. We've had peanut butter and jelly sandwiches for dinner for the last two nights. Tonight, we'll have rabbit stew."

Matt indicated her pickup. ''Any special reason you pulled up in front of my pumps?''

Charlie grimaced. ''I need some gas,'' she said, then, as Matt walked around to unscrew the gas cap, ''but I don't have any money.''

He continued as if he hadn't heard her. Charlie sat back in the cab, staring at the steering wheel, trying to decide if she ought to offer him an I.O.U.

When he returned to her window, she said, ''Would you get mad if I wrote you an I.O.U.?''

He nodded. ''Yep. So don't, okay?''

''Thanks, Matt.''

''You're welcome.'' He lowered his voice. ''John Foster told me about Red.''

Charlie looked away. ''That creep. At least he's gone.''

''Why didn't you come tell me?'' Gently, he reached over and brushed her cheek with his fingers. She winced away.

''Don't, Matt. And don't make a big thing about what happened. I'm okay.''

''But you didn't even *tell* me—''

''It wasn't any of your business,'' she said, looking straight at him.

''Okay, have it your way.'' He sighed, then changed the subject. ''Hey, tell you what, if you'd smile, I'd buy you dinner.''

''I'm busy,'' she said, starting the truck. ''I've got a date with a couple of skinned rabbits.''

''Thanks!'' he said, angry. ''I'm glad to know just how low I rank on your list, Charlie.'' He opened the pickup's door. ''Come on over here. I want to ask you something.''

''What?''

"Don't be so suspicious. I filled your gas tank, remember? You can act decent for ten seconds, can't you?"

Slowly, she turned off the Ford, got out of the cab and walked a few paces away with him. "What do you want?" she asked.

"I want to know how long you're gonna pretend that you can take care of yourself and bring those two kids up—peanut butter sandwiches for dinner—!" He sputtered to an indignant halt. "Charlie, you're gonna have to accept some more help than just a tank of gas. You can't do it!"

"I'm gonna do it!" she hissed back at him, "until Seth's eighteen! And if you don't like it, you can just get out of my life."

He glared at her, breathing heavily. "I *don't* like it."

"Then leave me alone from now on." She turned on her heel and marched back to the pickup, slamming the door so hard the ancient vehicle shook. She started the motor again.

Matt stood looking at her. "You mean that?"

"I mean it."

CHAPTER 9

Mrs. Daniels

Charlie managed to get the owner of the Happy Trails trailer park to give her a part-time job mowing the fields surrounding the place, washing down the rental trailers, filling in the potholes in the dirt road with gravel. It was backbreaking, thankless work, but Charlie was grateful to get it—until the owner, George Arnold Rhoades, put his arms around her one afternoon while Mrs. Rhoades was out shopping and made it clear that the real reason he'd hired her was that he expected her to earn the bulk of her pay horizontally. When Charlie told him "no," he laughed and tried to kiss her. Twenty seconds later Charlie was free and the balding little man was nursing a black eye, while Charlie told him what he could do with his generous offer—and reminded him that she was still under eighteen and that there were laws against what he had in mind.

But Rhoades had his revenge: a note attached to her next rental receipt informed Charlie that if her next week's rent was even a day late, she and her brothers would be evicted.

Christmas was less than two weeks away, and there would be no presents, no tree—and no place to live. Charlie drove out to the stockyards to ride, feeling as if the world were closing in on her. Even the big horse's easy strides across the mesa and the breathtaking panorama of the Davis Mountains to the north and Chinati Mountains to the southwest failed to soothe her, for once. She was backed into a corner, and she knew it.

She turned Sylvester and rode back, slowly, letting him pick his way through the twilight. She brushed him mechanically and put away her tack, climbed back into her truck, and drove home. Her gas tank was nearly empty again . . . and she'd die before she'd beg more from Matt.

Charlie walked into the trailer, trying to summon a smile, only to find Seth and Grant huddled together on the couch, their eyes wide and frightened. Grant—brash, sure-of-himself Grant—was near tears. "What happened?" Charlie said, her heart skipping a beat as she looked at them. "What's wrong?"

"Mrs. Daniels called while you were gone," Grant said, his eyes filling with tears. "She said she wants us to come in and see her tomorrow morning."

Charlie sank onto the couch, her arms going out to hug both boys. "Hey, don't get all upset, guys. It's probably nothing." She tried to think of something to say. "It's probably just that she wants you guys to sing in the Christmas chorus at church," she said, putting as much conviction as she could muster into her voice. "It's bound to be something like that."

Grant looked at her, and a tear broke free and slid down his freckled face. "You're a lousy liar, Charlie."

* * *

The next morning the three of them walked through the doors of the three-story Presidio County Courthouse promptly at nine. Charlie, who was wearing the only skirt she owned, fidgeted nervously with her half-slip. "Grant," she whispered, "look behind me and tell me is my slip hanging."

"Nope," he whispered back a moment later.

Charlie hesitated before the door marked, "Elizabeth Daniels—Child Welfare Supervisor," but finally knocked.

Mrs. Daniels opened the door after a second's pause. She was a short, plumpish woman whose dark eyes and hair marked her as being of mixed Indian and Mexican heritage. She wore a gray business suit. "Well, Charlie. You're here bright and early. Please step in."

The Railsbergs walked hesitantly into the office. Mrs. Daniels gestured them to seats. "Would you like a cup of coffee, Charlie?" she asked.

Charlie sat perched on the edge of the stiff tweed couch, her hands clasped white-knuckled in her lap. "No thank you, ma'am," she said.

Mrs. Daniels seated herself behind her huge oak desk, in front of the enormous Texas flag that hung behind her. Charlie thought that she'd never seen such a neat desk—there were no loose papers at all, just a single folder situated in the precise center of all that polished oak. Straining her eyes, she could read the names on the folder. "Railsberg," it read, "Grant and Seth."

"Well, Charlie, let's talk about why I asked you to come here," Mrs. Daniels said. "You haven't had much luck in finding a job, have you?"

Charlie forced herself to look directly at the woman. "No, ma'am."

"What do you plan to do about that?"

"Keep looking. I'll find something," she said, as confidently as she could manage.

"Well, you're certainly intelligent enough to get into something that pays well, like office work," Mrs. Daniels said. "I requested your school transcript, and it indicated you ought to be able to handle any of the courses at the vocational school. Perhaps a secretarial course . . ."

Charlie tensed. "I know what I want to do, Mrs. Daniels. And I'm good at it."

"And what is that, dear, aside from working around horses?"

She took a deep breath. "I'm *good* at breaking and training horses. That's not something everyone can do, believe me."

Mrs. Daniels raised her eyebrows, but didn't speak for nearly a minute. "Hmmmm. That's not really a *job,* is it, dear? That's just a phase you're going through. Nothing to be ashamed of, lots of girls have a 'horse-crazy' couple of years. But there comes a time when we all have to think about earning a living."

"That's what I want to do," Charlie said, through stiff lips. "I do it very well."

"But dear, there are no *jobs* in that area," Mrs. Daniels said with such reasonableness that Charlie wanted to leap over that enormous oaken desk and throttle her. "Now, I've signed you up for a course next semester. If you do well, this could open up a whole new range of jobs for you. Perhaps eventually even a computer course, over at Sul Ross State University, if the aptitude test shows promise . . ."

"What aptitude test?" Charlie demanded.

"The one I'd like you to come in and take. It will help us find out what you're best suited to do."

"I told you what I'm good at. I've spent four years learning how to do it right. That's the equivalent of going to college right there."

Mrs. Daniels smiled. "Now, the typing course I've signed you up for meets at—"

"Typing?" Charlie said blankly.

Mrs. Daniels's smile began to look a little tight at the edges. "Life is a highway, Charlene. We must approach each turn with enthusiasm and hope."

Charlie gave her a measuring look. "Can you make me take a typing course?"

Mrs. Daniels's smile looked as if it had been pasted on with glue. "I wish you'd consider me a friend, Charlene. I've heard about your attitude—"

"I asked you a question," Charlie broke in, her gaze flat and uncompromising.

Mrs. Daniels closed the file in front of her with a sigh. The smile was gone. "We can, yes. We've decided that it was a mistake to let you take on the burden of your family after your parents' death. When your cousin was staying with you that was one thing, but now . . ."

Charlie sat up straight on the couch, trying to keep alarm out of her voice. "So what does all this have to do with my taking a typing course?"

"We think it would be better for everyone concerned if you lived with a court-appointed guardian this year, while you take the secretarial course."

"*You*? Does that mean all of us? Or do you mean just *me*? What about my brothers?" Charlie tried to quell her rising panic.

"They have room for Grant and Seth at the Boys' Camp."

There, it was out—what she'd feared since last night. Charlie looked down at Seth and Grant. Both children stared up at her blankly, the panic she felt mirrored in their brown eyes. Charlie set her jaw stubbornly as she looked back up at the Child Welfare worker. "Forget it."

"You're only sixteen, Charlie—"

"Seventeen," she snapped.

"*Barely* seventeen," Mrs. Daniels amended. "You need time to discover yourself, unburdened by the terrible responsibilities you've undertaken these last couple of years. You need time to find out what you want—"

"I know what I want," Charlie said, tightly. "I want to keep my family together. I want to train horses. I *know* what I want!"

"But, Charlie, the work you've been doing is a dead-end job. Life as a wrangler is no life for someone with a family—it's not steady employment. And providing for a family of three is a financial and emotional burden for many adults—let alone someone your age."

"We help," Grant said. "I hunt, and last week I earned ten dollars working for Matt at the gas station."

"We eat rabbits," Seth said. "They don't even taste bad."

"I won't stay at Boys' Camp!" Grant cried.

"Me, too!" Seth's chubby little face was set in stubborn lines.

"It was harder when I was only fifteen, Mrs. Daniels," Charlie said. "Why now?"

"Well, dear, you're unemployed. And the benefits from your father's insurance have run out. It's the only way we can see to help you.'' She sighed. ''Be realistic, Charlie. You can't live on rabbits. And how are you going to pay your rent?''

Charlie hung her head. Her voice was low, anxious, as she twisted her hands in her lap. ''If I could have just a little more time, Mrs. Daniels. You have to admit that my brothers are healthy, and they're doing great in school. And I'm working on a project that will help me get established as a horse trainer. I'm training this horse for Mr. Foster, and he's really good. If I could train him so he sold for a real bundle, wouldn't that make training horses a real job?''

There was genuine regret in Mrs. Daniels's dark eyes. ''But, Charlie, you don't even work for John Foster anymore . . . try and put aside your antagonism, dear, and think about the boys. It's not like you won't get to see them ever again; you can go over on weekends.''

In silence, Charlie fought tears. Finally she found her voice, though she had to struggle to keep it normal. ''Grant's a part of me, and me him. And Seth . . . Seth means the world to us both. If you pull us apart—'' she stopped, because she couldn't continue.

Mrs. Daniels sighed, then tried a reassuring smile that didn't quite come off. ''You're all young. You'll be able to adjust. And remember, Charlie, when you've completed the course, and gotten a good job, you can probably receive full custody of your brothers again.'' She stood up. ''We'll be coming out to pick you up tomorrow, so please be packed.''

The three Railsbergs got up and left the office in silence.

When they were outside, walking toward the pickup parked across the square, Charlie heard a muffled sob from

Seth. She put a hard, calloused hand on the back of the little boy's neck, turning his tearful face up to her own as they walked. "Seth, she's probably watching us," she hissed fiercely. "So *don't*. Just *don't*."

"But Charlie—" he tried to control himself.

"I'll think of something," she promised him. "I *will*."

But she couldn't imagine what.

CHAPTER 10

Night Moves

''Couldn't you marry Matt?'' Grant asked, half sitting up in his narrow bed in the trailer. Seth lay on the other bed, asleep, snoring like a puppy. It was very late.

Charlie rolled her eyes. ''*No*. That's about the tackiest thing I've ever heard you say, Grant. You don't marry somebody just to get out of trouble.''

''Mom did,'' Grant said soberly. ''She was gonna have *you*.''

''Who told you that?'' Charlie demanded.

''I heard Mrs. Stewart say so to Mrs. Lopez. Was it true, Charlie?''

Charlie bit her lip. ''That was a long time ago, Grant, and I'm sure if Momma had wanted you to know about that, she'd have told you herself.''

''Did she tell *you?*''

''None of your business. The point is, I'm not gonna marry anybody.''

"So what do we do tomorrow? Just go with 'em? I'm telling you, Charlie, I'll run away. I won't stay there. That place is like a prison."

"You do that, and I'll never be able to get custody of you two again. It won't be that long, Grant . . . maybe just a year or so." She tried to force conviction into her voice. "Mrs. Daniels is right . . . we can't live on rabbits, and I *don't* have a job. I've been thinking about what she said, and I wish you'd try to see it that way . . . life is a highway, and we have to—"

"I wish *you'd* go pee up a tree, Charlie!" Grant burst out, then began to sob.

Wordlessly, she reached over to hug him. His strong little arms clutched hard around her neck in return.

Grant was still sniffling when Charlie suddenly stiffened, sitting up on the floor by his bed so abruptly that she bumped his chin with the top of her head. "Uuumph!" he cried.

Charlie rubbed the top of her head automatically, though she scarcely felt the pain. "Grant, I know what to do! I've got a plan! Wake Seth up, and the two of you get dressed!"

Two hours later Charlie's Ford pickup, loaded with the Railsbergs' possessions, including the mattresses from their beds, pulled away from the Happy Trails Mobile Home Park. Charlie had scrounged up a can of gasoline from Rhoades's storage barn and tipped its contents into her own gas tank. Rhoades, she figured, owed her at least that much on the three days' rent she still had coming on the Schultz.

"Where are we going, Charlie?" Seth asked sleepily, bundled into his down jacket. Winters in Marfa seldom saw snow before January, but the ground beneath the full moon was silvered by frost.

"Mr. Foster's house," Charlie said, as they pulled bumpily out onto the main road. They drove in silence to the stockyards, then continued past them on the rutted old dirt road leading to John Foster's place.

"You ever been here before?" whispered Grant.

"Once," Charlie replied. "I came over with Matt when he had some feed to drop off."

The pickup rolled to a halt before a squat, one-story house with a formerly whitewashed adobe front. A sagging porch poked out from its front, shadowed by huge oaks looming in the yard. A large, stone-walled barn stood off to one side, and Charlie could see the edge of a fence. Farther away, a water tank and a windmill took on eerie, alien shapes in the silver-blue moonlight.

The unlighted house crouched before them. Charlie turned off the ignition. "He's not here," Grant whispered.

"His truck is," Charlie said.

"Then he's asleep," Grant warned.

Charlie swung her door open. "We're gonna wake him up, then."

Leaving the boys in the truck, she walked up to the door, nearly tripping over a chair on the porch. Gathering her nerve, she knocked.

Silence.

Charlie knocked again, louder. Finally a light flashed on inside the house, and she could hear the sound of shuffling feet. John Foster, clad in a maroon gabardine robe pulled over pajamas, peered out the front doorway. His eyes were bloodshot and he swayed slightly as he stood. It took him all of half a minute to recognize Charlie.

She made a frustrated gesture as she flinched away from the assault of his breath. It was a smell she recognized only too well. "Are you drunk? Lord, what a mess! You're as bad as my Dad. *Rats*." Angrily, she headed back across the porch toward the yard.

"What is this?" Foster stumbled after her, confused. "What's going on?"

Charlie kept walking. "I needed to talk to you. I *needed* you, period. And you're *drunk!*"

Foster, stung, stopped on the edge of the porch, eyeing the pickup crammed with suitcases and worn household furnishings. "I'm always drunk!"

Charlie's voice overflowed with sarcasm. "Well, lucky you." She reached the cab of the pickup and spoke to Grant and Seth. "Come on, guys. I made a mistake. We'll head for Oklahoma."

She got in, slamming the door, so frustrated and despairing that she wanted to fling herself down on the ground and either cry or sleep—whichever came first. Foster, beginning now to wake up, followed her over to the opposite side of the pickup and looked in. "Hello, son," he said to Seth. The smaller boy was leaning against Grant, who held his head in a comforting—if uncomfortable—armlock.

"We've got some folks somewhere in Oklahoma," Charlie snarled, fumbling for her keyring. "At least they were still there last Christmas. That'll be better than living with a drunk. Me and Grant had enough of living with a drunk to last us a lifetime, while Daddy was alive."

Foster blinked, comprehension finally beginning to sink into his clouded brain. "You were thinking of living with *this* drunk?"

"It'd be better than going to Boys' Camp," Grant said. "We could earn our keep. I can shoot rabbits and do chores . . . she can cook."

"Sort of," amended Seth. "Stew, anyhow."

"Seth!" Charlie said, reproachfully.

Foster was not listening. He shook his head, pursing his lips. "I finished raising kids ten years ago."

"We don't want to stay with you anyway, now," Charlie snapped.

"I don't have the room," Foster said.

"We could stay in the barn," Grant said. "We've got down-filled sleeping bags."

Charlie turned on the boy, fiercely. "We're *not* moving in with a drunk!"

Seth suddenly twisted out of Grant's hold, pushing open his door. He jumped out of the pickup, raced up the path to the house, and disappeared in the front door.

After a stunned second, Charlie and Grant ran after him. They found themselves in a small living room adjoining a kitchen. Through a door they could see into a miniscule bedroom. The bathroom was a curtained alcove off the living room with an old-fashioned claw-footed tub.

Charlie stared at the place in near-horror. She'd never seen such a mess in her life. It was a pack rat's nest to make the one in Foster's office look like a paragon of spacious neatness. Stacks of yellowing magazines encased the furniture on three sides, sometimes towering four feet into the air. The walls were a jumbled rainbow of colors from where they'd been plastered and repainted full decades ago. A yellowed cavalry recruiting poster sagged drunkenly over the couch, which dipped in the middle as though it had decided the poster had the right idea. Two split-seated McClellan Army saddles occupied the back of the only armchair, their boxy stirrups draped across the tattered antimacassars festooning its arms. The only bookshelf held bottles of whiskey, some empty, many not.

Two motheaten stuffed animals, a coyote and a spotted antelope buck, stared glassily out from opposite corners of the room. Even to the untrained eye, they represented amateur attempts at taxidermy.

Seth was sitting on the corner of the couch, staring around him. "This place is *amazing,*" he announced solemnly as they stood in the doorway. "Nobody makes *him* clean up his room."

"What are you doing?" demanded Foster.

"Moving in with a drunk," Seth answered. He yawned suddenly, hugely.

"Seth, I'm going to count to three," Charlie announced. "You get over here. One—"

"I don't want to go to Oklahoma either, Charlie," Grant interrupted. He sat down on the coffee table, nearly tipping over a huge Chinese red ashtray filled with pipe dottles and matchsticks.

John Foster moved over to the bookshelf and poured himself a stiff jolt of whiskey. He turned back to look at them, the glass in his hand. "Can we stay with you?" Seth asked, blinking sleepily. "Please?"

"For tonight at least?" Grant said.

"Please?" Seth rested his head tiredly on his arm.

For a long moment, nobody moved or spoke. Then Charlie nodded at Grant, her mouth tight. "Go start putting the stuff in the barn. He doesn't mind."

Grant and Seth bolted out the door, the smaller boy's excitement at being allowed to stay overcoming his exhaustion—at least temporarily. Charlie stared at John Foster for another long moment. The old man's eyes slid away from hers, then he knocked back the whiskey with a practiced snap of his wrist that ended Charlie's last lingering doubt as to whether she'd caught Foster in a rare overindulgence—he did this often. The man lowered his empty glass, his tired old eyes watering a little. "This is a mistake," he announced, his voice graveled from the liquor.

"You're telling me," Charlie said. She turned on her heel and marched out of the house, to begin helping the boys with their gear.

Foster's barn proved to be in better shape than the house: it was tight and weatherproof, with a wood-floored section where they set their beds. They found a collection of old furniture in one corner, and located two bunk beds. They set them up, then pulled Grant's and Seth's mattresses up onto them. Charlie piled her mattress on top of a rusty set of springs she dragged out of a corner. They moved bales of straw to block off the draft from under the door. There was even a wall socket where they could plug in a lamp. Snug in their down sleeping bags, the Railsbergs finally drifted off to sleep to the accompaniment of the soft whufflings of Gladys, Foster's white mule, and two dairy cows working their cuds.

The next morning, Charlie and the boys went up to the house to clean up. John Foster was already up and dressed, though Charlie suspected from his expression that he was nursing a pounding headache. "Eggs and bacon in the fridge," he said, jerking a thumb at the kitchen. "Make sure those boys drink some of that orange juice I fixed.

School bus stops up at the main highway, by the Interstate sign."

Charlie hesitated, not knowing what to say. Foster picked his hat off the rack and slung his down vest over his shoulder. "I could use some help at the yards today, if you've got nothin' better planned. Got a load of goats in yesterday for auction."

Slowly a grin spread over her face, and she nodded. "I'll be there." *One day at a time,* she thought. *One thing at a time. I'll be able to talk to him about hiring me back . . . maybe I can even call Mrs. Daniels to tell her I'm working again . . .*

"Good." Foster looked at Seth and Grant, who were busily exploring the contents of his refrigerator, and shuddered as he went out.

Ray Johnson, the auctioneer, twanged his nearly incomprehensible litany of bids as Charlie, mounted on Sylvester, herded twenty-five Nubian goats around the auction ring. John Foster sat by the exit gate, ready to open it when the goats were sold. Charlie was grinning despite the dust and noise because it felt so great to be riding the gray gelding again. She patted his neck as he minced after the goats, his ears flicking forward then back as he listened to his rider and the noise of the crowd.

"This is good practice for you, Sylvester," she said. "In a show ring, it's almost like this, only there are lots of other horses and riders around. I'll have to see if I can't borrow a trailer and take you to some local shows, just so you can get used to them—"

Charlie broke off her one-sided conversation as she looked past Foster to the entrance and saw Elizabeth Daniels, looking terribly out-of-place in a suit and hat, accompanied by Captain Stanley Marsh of the Marfa police force. They were watching her, their expressions grim.

Foster noticed her frozen stare and turned to see Marsh and Mrs. Daniels as they picked their way through the crowd. The old man turned back to Charlie, and the two of them looked at each other for a long moment.

"Hey, John?" Ray's voice boomed, amplified by the microphone. "These here goats have been sold. You want to move them out?"

Foster started, then opened the gate. Charlie, feeling as though her face had been carved out of ice, herded the Nubians through it. Her mind wasn't on her work, and several times she had to send Sylvester racing after one of the frisky little creatures. Finally she managed to herd them into their new owner's truck, and turned back to the auction barn.

Foster, Captain Marsh, and Mrs. Daniels were talking outside the entrance. As Charlie rode up, the old man jerked his thumb at Appy, who, as relief stock horse, was standing tied to the hitching rail with his saddle on, dozing in the pale winter sunlight.

"Charlie, Captain Marsh here has a kid who rides rodeo, and needs a faster pony. I been tellin' him about Appy."

She looked into the old man's blue eyes, seeing one of them close in a quick wink. "Oh, yessir. He's nice and quick, Appy is. Trained him myself, and he can do just about anything and do it right."

"What?" Stanley Marsh looked from Charlie to Foster, taken aback. "John, no, I can't—"

Mrs. Daniels said, at the same moment, "Now Mr.

Foster, we're not here to make any horse deals. We're here to—''

Foster raised his voice to be heard over both of them. ''So I want you to take the Captain out back to the stock pens, Charlie, and sell him that pony. Understand?''

''Yessir!'' Charlie hooked her right leg over the saddle-horn and swung off Sylvester, handing the gray's reins to Foster. Grabbing Appy's bridle off the rail, she slipped the bit into the little horse's mouth. ''See, Captain Marsh? He's real easy to saddle and bridle . . . perfect for a youth horse.''

''Charlene!'' Mrs. Daniels fussed. ''You'll do no such thing. Now Captain Marsh and I have come to talk to you about—'' she glared up at Foster. ''John, this is official business. Could we please use your office?''

''Of course,'' he said, taking her arm, ''we'll go up and have some coffee and a nice talk while Captain Marsh and Charlie here play cowboy. I want you to give me the forms I need to act as guardian for the Railsberg kids.''

Charlie sucked in a surprised breath, but after a second, continued tightening Appy's girth as though she'd known about it all along.

''Guardian!'' Mrs. Daniels was flabbergasted. ''Why, John, you'd never be approved!''

''Why not?'' he asked.

Mrs. Daniels looked at the crowds of people coming and going in and out of the auction barn. ''Can't we use your office?''

''*Why not?*''

Her lips tightened. ''You're too old, you're unmarried, and you're a drunk, John.''

''Aside from that,'' Charlie said, feeling her heart skidding around in her chest like a weanling colt. She didn't know whether to giggle or sob. Maybe both.

"You get on!" Foster took Mrs. Daniels by the arm. "Sell him that horse!"

"Here you go, Captain Marsh," Charlie said, "just put your foot in this stirrup like this—" Deftly she lifted the portly man's left foot into the stirrup, then boosted. The stunned Marsh found himself astride the little Appaloosa before he knew what was happening. Charlie adjusted the stirrups, chattering on about the pony's abilities.

"Now," Charlie said, tying Sylvester to the hitching rail, "let's go find some cows."

Leading Appy, she towed the middle-aged police captain toward the stock pens.

As she opened the gate into the calf pen, Marsh looked uneasy. "You know, Charlie, I haven't ridden in twenty years. I really ought to bring Tim—"

"Now don't you worry, Captain. Appy is so well trained he barely even needs a rider by now. You see that calf with the crooked horn?" She pointed. Marsh nodded. "Well, you just nudge this little guy toward that calf, and let him do the rest."

She stepped back, whacking the horse with the palm of her hand. Appy leaped forward, nearly unseating the officer, who yelped and grabbed the horn. After a second, Marsh reined him in the direction of the brindled little calf, and Appy went into action, ears plastered against his head, snorting.

The calf ducked and turned, racing to try and get back with the bunch, but Appy separated it from the rest of its fellows with the precision of a surgeon using a scalpel and kept it at bay, weaving and plunging entirely on his own. Captain Marsh had completely abandoned the reins and was clinging to the saddle with both hands, his eyes wide with amazement. Finally Charlie whistled. "Enough! Rein him away, Captain, before you give that calf a nervous breakdown!"

Clumsily, Marsh reined away the Appaloosa, and Appy jogged smoothly over to Charlie, who laughed, kissed his nose, and rubbed him behind the ears. "He's 'bout as good at roping and reining as he is at cutting, Captain Marsh. What do you think?"

The portly officer climbed off, his legs sagging a bit as they encountered *terra firma* again. "*You* trained this horse, Charlie?"

She laughed proudly. "Yes, sir. I was the first person ever to ride him, and it took me nearly two years. And Mrs. Daniels wants to turn me into a secretary."

Marsh frowned. "Well, you can tell Foster I'll bring my trailer by this afternoon when I get off duty. Tim is gonna love this little horse. Also," he rubbed the Appaloosa's black-spotted head, "you tell Foster that I'm gonna pay him a decent price, and that I want some of it to go to you for a commission. Okay?"

Charlie shook her head. "I don't want a commission. I just want you to talk Mrs. Daniels into letting us stay with him."

Marsh hesitated. "There's nothing wrong with being a secretary, Charlie."

She scratched Appy's neck, smiling as he closed his eyes contentedly. "I don't *want* to be a secretary. It's not what I was cut out to do, and if you're honest, Captain, you'll tell Mrs. Daniels so."

* * *

John Foster handed Elizabeth Daniels a cup of coffee. She took it gingerly, then set it on the edge of his desk. Foster stood in front of her, his expression intense, watchful. "I meant what I said, Betty. Help me do it."

She looked up at him, raising her eyebrows. "After not informing us of their whereabouts, you expect us to bend rules for you?"

"I notice you didn't have much trouble finding them," Foster said. "That girl's had it rough. I want to help her out. I've given her her job back."

Mrs. Daniels sniffed. "Charlie needs a more suitable profession, John. Breaking horses isn't what one could term stable employment—if you'll pardon the pun. And Boys' Camp is a fine place. She could take a secretarial course, get a good job, then have Grant and Seth moved back to her custody."

"It's a crime to separate them!" Foster said, slamming a fist into his palm. "I saw that last night. Those kids are close, Betty. *Close*."

"It's a crime not to, John," she replied.

He glared at her. "Well, make sure you bring the militia when you come out to get 'em."

She stood, nearly knocking the cup of coffee over in her anger. "Are you telling me you are going to deliberately violate—"

"I'm telling you that I'm keeping those kids. I'll sign whatever's necessary, do whatever I have to."

"Even quit drinking?" she challenged.

"Yeah," he said, after a moment. "Yeah, I would."

"Why are you doing this, John?"

He turned away, staring out the grimy window at nothing. "Let's say I owe it to someone."

CHAPTER 11

Bless This House . . .

Matt Grey was sitting in his office at Webb's, watching a *M.A.S.H.* rerun on his little black-and-white and picking his teeth when the battered Ford pickup jolted up onto the apron and parked outside the office. Matt sat up, turning off the set, tossing the toothpick into the trash as he watched Charlie Railsberg come in the door. He did his best to look casually unconcerned. "Hi, Charlie. How's it going?"

"Much better, Matt," she said, digging several crumpled bills out of her jeans. "I came to pay you for the gas and pick up Grant."

"You don't owe me any—" he began to protest, then his eyes widened as he saw her stuff a ten back into her pocket, leaving two fives and three ones on the desk. "What'd you do, rob a bank? Last I knew, you didn't have two dimes to rub together."

"Mr. Foster gave me my job back, and advanced me

some salary. We're living out at his place now, in the barn."

"In the *barn?* Isn't that kinda chilly?"

"Well, we did all right last night, and I have one of those electric heaters I can plug in. But . . ." she bit her lip, "I sort of wanted to ask you if you'd mind helping me . . ."

"Help you with what?"

"I'll need to build a brick place for it to stand, 'cause there's a wooden floor where we're sleeping. Can you help, Matt?"

Matt tried to hold back a grin, failed. "Yeah, you know I will. I'll be out tomorrow."

Charlie grinned back. "Thanks, Matt. I'm glad we're back on speaking terms . . . I hated fighting with you." She hesitated. "I missed you."

"Tell me about it." He stepped closer to her, and, for once, she didn't back away. Matt wanted to touch her cheek again, but restrained himself. It was enough that she'd come back to make up with him. "So, you're gonna do Christmas all the way this year, huh?"

"What?" she frowned.

"Spend it in a stable," he explained.

She made a face at him, then chuckled. "See you later. I've got a lot of work to do out at Foster's. That house is a *mess*. Grant in the service bay?"

"Yeah."

"Grant!" she yelled, and a second later the ten-year-old came around the corner and hopped into the pickup.

"See you tomorrow!" she called, heading for the truck.

"Bye," he said from the doorway. "Merry Christmas!"

She turned back from the cab of the Ford to give him a

brilliant smile, her blue-gray eyes sparkling. "Same to you, Matt."

John Foster drove his pickup into his yard, seeing Charlie's Ford parked by the barn. He looked over at the house, noting that all the lights were lit in the early December night. Rock 'n' roll drifted faintly out into the darkness beneath the oaks. Foster sighed, then, after a second, got out of the truck. He was tired; his steps toward the kitchen light were slow.

When he opened the door, he stared around the house, his eyes widening. The place had been transformed. All the stacks of newspapers were gone, the coyote and antelope had vanished, the saddles were hung neatly on the saddle racks in the corner.

The furniture shone faintly from energetic dusting, the carpet was clean, and the poster had been put back up. The empty whiskey bottles were gone, and the old family dining table had been rescued from the barn and stood just outside the kitchen, the rickety chairs ranged around it. Seth sat at the table, drawing, and Grant looked up from another seat where he was cleaning one of Foster's old .22's. Charlie was dishing something onto plates in the kitchen.

My place doesn't belong to me, anymore, the old man thought, taking in all the changes. *Who told them they could do this to me? To my house?* Aloud he snapped, "Turn off that noise!"

Seth hastily turned off the radio. Both boys looked at him, frightened by his tone—which only made Foster more irritated. "Is that my gun?" he barked at Grant.

"Yessir," the older boy said. "It hadn't been cleaned in a hundred years—"

Foster reached out to take it, put it back up onto the gun rack. "I *like* it dirty." Grant nodded, wide-eyed. The man gestured at the table and chairs, pacing back and forth like an old lion. "This all went into the barn for a reason, did that ever occur to you?"

"Seth needed a place to draw," Grant said.

"And we needed a place to eat together," called Charlie from the kitchen. "Grant and Seth, move your things. I'm almost ready to bring the plates out."

"How'd you fix the chairs?" demanded Foster, looking suspiciously down at the old straight-backs.

"Krazy Glue," Grant said, moving his things off the table.

"It won't hold," Foster said, taking off his vest and hat.

Charlie came out with four bowls of chicken stew, two in each hand. "Grant, go get the cornbread and green beans." She looked over at the old man as she set the food down at each place. "Quit being such a grouch, Mr. Foster. Sit. Eat."

Hesitantly Foster sat, adjusting his position in the chair gingerly. "You keep a civil tongue in your head, Charlie," he growled, picking up his fork and starting to eat. The stew was hot and tasty, and he hadn't realized how hungry he was until he began eating.

"We'll put it all back," Grant promised, sitting with his hands folded in front of him.

Charlie gave Foster, who was still eating steadily, a pointed glance as she also folded her hands. "Go ahead, Seth."

"God, Mr. Foster has a mule named Gladys who is my new best friend. Thanks for not making us go to Oklahoma. Give Mom a hug. Amen," the little boy said.

Foster ate, not looking up.

After a minute or two, Charlie looked up, swallowed, and said brightly, "Grant got two more rabbits and three quail today, Mr. Foster."

Grant nodded, forgetting some of his worry in the memory of his accomplishment. "Yeah, you know how little quail are? It's like shooting a little dot."

"*And,*" Charlie gave the older boy a fond glance, "he earned five dollars working for Matt at the gas station after school."

Foster glared at her. "You trying to sell him to me?"

Grant looked down at his plate, obviously embarrassed, then shrugged. "We found some bunks for me and Seth out in the barn last night, Mr. Foster. Is that all right with you?"

"None of this is all right with me," the old man said, feeling like Scrooge, but unable to stop himself. His age-veined hand moved over the table, caressing the dryness of the neglected wood. "I should've moved into the Herring Hotel when Irene died. I should've burned this. *And* those bunks."

Panicked glances ran around the table between Charlie and her brothers. Seth looked over at him, his chubby little features anxious. "Don't you like kids?"

"I don't even like my own kids!" Foster looked away from Seth.

"Why not?" the little boy asked.

"Because they're not worth liking!" Foster said, feeling

totally put on the defensive, which infuriated him—here, in his own house, of all places!

Grant broke his cornbread and buttered it, not looking up. "Ben Daniels said your son killed somebody."

"Grant!" Charlie cried. "You're worse than Seth! Where are your manners?"

Mention of John Junior had driven away the remainder of Foster's appetite. He wiped his mouth with short, jerky motions and stood. "I'm going into town."

He put on his down vest, then turned to find them all sitting perfectly still, watching him in silent fear. He shook his head. "I don't think this is going to work, Charlie."

"You haven't given us a chance," she said quietly.

Foster picked up his keys. "I'm too old, too set in my ways."

"Too hateful," Grant said, his brown eyes accusing. Charlie kicked at him, caught the chair, and it broke under the boy, depositing him on the floor with a thump. He lay glaring up at the old man, furious.

John Foster picked up his hat. "And too hateful. Exactly."

He walked out, leaving them staring after him.

Quanch's Bar was doing a brisk business. Foster saw Matt Grey's pickup nosed into the curb, and he found Matt himself sitting at the bar, drinking a beer, when he entered. The dark-haired youth was watching the Sul Ross football team with Steve, the middle-aged bartender.

The black-and-yellow clad players of Tarleton State scrambled after the crimson and gray of the Sul Ross quarterback, who lobbed a hasty, overthrown pass at the nearest receiver, only to have it intercepted. "Look at that turkey wearing your number, Matt!'' Steve exclaimed. ''If I was you I'd kick his rear for playing like that while he's wearing it!''

Matt shrugged and took a sip of Coors. ''Ahhh, he's all right. Just needs more experience so he'll learn to keep his cool.''

''You coulda been a pro, Matt. Why'd you quit?''

The young man shrugged, turning away from the bartender, then saw Foster across the room and waved him over. ''What'll it be, John?'' Steve asked.

''Beer, Steve. And bring another for James Dean over here.'' Foster clapped Matt on the shoulder of his black leather jacket as he sat down beside him.

''Sure thing,'' Steve said.

Matt gave Foster a wry grin. ''I'm right ticked off that she went to you 'stead of me, John.''

''Me too,'' Foster agreed dryly. They both laughed, and Foster felt the tensions of the day begin to slip away. He remembered how he'd acted toward the Railsberg boy, and grimaced as he sipped the beer Steve handed him. It felt cold and bitterly good in his mouth.

Steve was still standing opposite them at the bar, idly polishing it with a towel. ''They say you got the Railsberg kids, John.''

''Not for long,'' Foster said, grimly, wondering if he really would kick them out. *Why me?* he wondered grumpily.

''Over the objections of the City of Marfa and the State of Texas, I hear you applied for legal guardianship. That's something, all right.''

Matt Grey laughed. ''Kicking Mrs. Daniels's butt was something. 'Bout time somebody told her she doesn't run heaven and earth.'' He toasted Foster with his Coors and took a swallow.

Steve grinned lewdly. "I'll say. And that Charlene Railsberg sure is something, too!" He wriggled his eyebrows and made a lip-smacking noise.

Foster and Matt froze, staring at him coldly. "I beg your pardon?" the older man said, after a second.

Steve, oblivious to the tone in John's voice, continued confidingly, "I woulda hired her in a minute—she'd draw boys like flies to honey with one twitch of those nice little buns of hers. Pretty gal. But she's underage." He mopped at the bar and gave Foster a sharp, knowing glance. "Her mother was a friend of yours too, wasn't she, John?"

The old man took a slow, deliberate swallow. "She was." He put the mug down and stared levelly at the bartender.

"*More* than a friend?" suggested Steve.

"Steve," Matt Grey said warningly.

The bartender ignored the younger man.

"What does that have to do with the present situation?" Foster asked, tonelessly.

"Well . . ." Steve shrugged mock-innocently. "You know how people talk."

"Are you suggesting—" Matt's body was taut beneath the black leather.

The bartender shrugged again. "Well, she looks a lot like her mother. She's ripe. And his house," he jerked his thumb at Foster, "is back off the road. Only *one* bedroom—" He broke off, still grinning, as Matt grabbed the front of his shirt with both hands and jerked him against the bar. He waved his hands in surrender, laughing harder. "Hey, don't get sore at me! I don't start the rumors, I just keep 'em going—"

His words broke off as Matt reared back and slugged

him on the jaw. Steve's eyes turned glassy, and, as Matt let him go, he sank down onto the floor behind the bar.

Neither Foster nor Matt (or anyone else in Quanch's) noticed. They were too busy staring at the bar as they drank their beer in silence. Finally Foster sighed. "I was going to boot 'em out tomorrow."

"You can't do that," Matt said flatly.

"She's got family in Oklahoma."

The young man's dark eyes held the older man's blue ones for a long moment before Matt spoke. "I don't want her in Oklahoma, John."

Foster's tone was dry. "You don't, huh?"

"I'm waiting on Charlie to get this horse training stuff out of her system and grow up, John. Then I'm fixing to marry her."

Foster nodded, sipping at his beer. "I remember when we were breaking mules in the Army, the jennies were every one of them harder to gentle, but once you had their attention, there wasn't a thing in the world they wouldn't do for you."

He turned to look at Matt as he took another drink. "The jacks'd get tired, get cranky, then they'd quit on you. The jennies were the ones with heart."

Matt laughed a little, shaking his head. "Are you saying I got my eye on a mule, John?"

The older man smiled. "I'm saying if it takes awhile, it's probably worth it."

"Or would be . . . if she were a mule." Matt was grinning now.

"Right," Foster agreed, taking another swallow. They laughed. "You're a good kid, Matt," the older man said. "Steady and dependable. She'll need someone like you when she's ready to settle down. Someone who won't dump sand on her spirit, trying to put it out, like her Daddy did to Lena."

"So you did know her mother?"

"Oh, yeah, I knew her. Lena was about four when I left home to join the Army, and I knew her Dad real well. I used to see her sometimes, when I'd come home on leave, bring her little things from wherever I'd been stationed. Then I didn't get home for about eight years, and when I did—" he shook his head, his eyes shadowed at the memory, "why, Lena was all grown up, and beautiful—Lord, she was beautiful! She was also married to Railsberg and already had Charlie."

"Did she remember you?"

"Yup." Foster finished his beer.

A hand appeared over the bar and Steve pulled himself up, shakily, leaning on the counter to rub gingerly at the side of his face.

"Well, hello," Foster said. "Have a nice nap?" Steve eyed both of them warily. "Now you listen carefully, Steve. This is for publication. The Railsberg kids are living in my *barn*. The girl cooks, the bigger boy works at Webb's for Matt, and the little boy looks after my mule." He smiled. "If anyone suggests otherwise, take their name, Steve. Matt here'll straighten them out."

The man nodded as fervently as his swelling jaw would allow. "Right."

"And Steve—" the bartender had turned to leave.

"Sir," said Steve, turning back.

"If *you* suggest otherwise, be sure your life insurance is paid up."

Steve worked his jaw. "John, I got your drift."

"Good. Then bring me a bottle of Jose Cuervo."

Matt looked over at Foster as the older man tipped the whiskey into a shot glass and knocked it back. "I thought you quit drinking real whiskey."

"I quit when my kids left," Foster wiped his mouth. "Now I got me a new batch."

Charlie awakened to the sound of a truck's engine. Groggily she sat up in her sleeping bag in the barn, groping for the old wind-up alarm clock with the luminous dial. "What time is it?" asked Grant, sleepily.

"Two-thirty," she said, putting the clock back. They lay in their beds, listening, as Foster's steps thumped unsteadily up to the front door, then came the sound of a muffled crash as the old man must've fallen over one of the Krazy-Glued chairs. A slurred but colorful cacophony of purple expressions followed, loud in the night's stillness.

"Wow," whispered Seth, "he sure knows a lot of bad words!"

"Don't you listen, Seth," Charlie snapped. "Put your hands over your ears."

Another crash resounded from the house, then the sound of a flushing toilet. "Remember when Daddy came home from the oilfields?" Grant said, in a hushed voice.

"Yup," Charlie replied.

"Remember the time he broke Mom's arm?"

"Yup."

"Do you think he'll come out here?" Seth asked, in a small voice.

"I don't think so," Charlie said, trying to put confidence into her voice. She really *didn't* think Foster would hurt them—but she'd been wrong before, about her own father . . .

"You scared, Grant?" Seth said.

Grant was quiet in the darkness for a second, before he responded, "Yup."

"I'm not," Charlie said firmly. "Mr. Foster's a good man."

"So was Daddy, when he wasn't drinking," Grant said.

The Railsbergs listened in the darkness for footsteps coming toward the barn—and Charlie's heart bounced against her ribs when she heard the front door open again. But then there was only silence, until they heard a regular squeak . . . squeak . . . squeak . . .

"What's he doing?" Charlie asked.

Grant, who was in the top bunk, rustled as he crawled to look out of the hairline crack in the barn wall. "He's sitting in the rocking chair, with the cat in his lap."

"Her name's Pearl," Seth supplied.

"Oh," Charlie whispered, snuggling back into her sleeping bag. "Grant, lie down before you catch your death."

As Charlie drifted toward sleep again, she heard the old man's voice, singing softly:

"If you don't love me, love whom you please.
Throw your arms round me, give my heart ease.
Give my heart ease, love, give my heart ease,
Throw your arms round me, give my heart ease."

CHAPTER 12

Silver Bells, Golden Rings

"Dear God," Grant said into his folded hands, "please bless this Christmas dinner Charlie worked so hard to fix, and bless all of us at this table. Thanks for letting us stay together, and bless Mom, too. Thanks for the fishing pole! Amen."

"Amen," the Railsbergs echoed, John Foster's graveled tones a beat behind. The old man picked up the staghorn-handled knife and fork and began carving vigorously.

"I hope it's okay," Charlie said nervously. "First time I ever cooked anything that big."

"I want a drumstick!" shouted Seth.

"Wait your turn, young man," Foster said, mock-severely, deftly slicing off a drumstick and lowering a slab of it onto the little boy's plate.

"Yummy!" he mumbled around a mouthful, not standing on ceremony while the others were served.

"Don't talk with your mouth full, Seth," Charlie

admonished, watching Foster anxiously as he chewed his first bite of turkey and gravy.

"Not bad," the old man said thoughtfully, after a moment, "not bad at all. And it ain't stew."

Charlie made a face at him, grinned, then began eating.

Dinner was over and she was washing dishes, while Grant dried, when there was a knock at the kitchen door. "Come in," she called, wondering who could be visiting Foster today; he had turned surly on her when she'd asked if he'd be seeing any of his family over the holiday.

"Hi, Merry Christmas!" Matt Grey said, coming in and taking off his hat and vest. A large plastic garbage bag at his feet bulged with intriguing lumps and bumps.

"Merry Christmas yourself," Charlie said. "Have you eaten? I haven't put the turkey away yet."

"Well, Mom fixed dinner for all of us, but it's been an hour or so," Matt said, and without further invitation carved himself a generous slice.

"For goodness sake put it on a plate!" Charlie fussed.

"Why?" asked Matt, swallowing and starting on the next bite. "That'd just dirty another dish. Hey, this is good. Any gravy left?"

"Matt!" Seth raced in from the back door. "Have you got a present for me?"

"Seth!"

"That's okay," Matt chuckled, fishing in the bag. "Sure have, amigo. Here you go. Have fun."

Wrapping paper went flying as the boy tore the package open. "Matt! He-Man and the Dragonwalker! This is great!" The little boy ripped the plastic covering off the action figure. "Thanks!"

"You're welcome," Matt replied, but Seth was already

gone, producing Dragonwalker (what, in Heaven's name, Charlie wondered, was a *Dragonwalker?*) noises at a pitch and volume that made them all cringe.

"And for my young sportsman here . . ." Matt fished in the bag for a long, slender package. "Here you go."

Grant's fingers tore excitedly at the gaily colored paper and ragged curliques of ribbon. Finally he had the package open, staring in amazement at the shining wood and blued steel of the weapon. "Matt—a double-barrel two-ten! Wow! Just what I wanted!"

"Mind you remember the rules," Matt admonished. "You can only use it if I go out with you. I don't want to catch you knocking birds out of trees or scaring Foster's cattle. You've got to remember that a gun of your own is a big responsibility. And when Seth is around, it stays locked in the gun rack. Understand?"

"Yes," Grant said, nodding soberly, only his eyes alight. "I understand, Matt. I won't even clean it when Seth's around, I promise. Thanks, Matt!" For a moment Charlie thought the boy might throw his arms around the young man, but after a second he contented himself with pumping Matt's hand. The adult gesture from the small figure made her eyes sting. *Lordy, he's growing up so fast!* she thought.

After Grant had left to show Foster his treasure, Matt turned to Charlie. "I think there's something more in the bag, but you'll have to step out on the porch to get it."

"Wait a second till I get yours," she said, wiping her hands on the dishtowel. She came back in a moment with a package. After handing it to Matt, Charlie shrugged into a heavy red-and-black checked wool shirt against the chill after sunset, then they walked out onto the front porch.

The oaks rustled softly in the yard, and in the distance, Charlie could hear the sounds of the Dragonwalker (*à la* Seth). Matt rested a hip against the porch railing as he pulled at the wrappings of his present. Charlie suddenly wished she'd gotten something more for him, but most of her pay had gone toward the boys' presents and a new hatband for Foster. "It's socks," she blurted, unable to stand the suspense as Matt slowly untied the bow, separated the paper. "They've got battery connections, and they keep your feet warm like an electric blanket. For hunting, or working outside."

"Hey, all right!" Matt admired the footwear. "How'd you know red's my favorite color?"

"You told me last year."

"Well, thanks. These will come in handy next cold spell. We're bound to get some snow in January and February."

"I wish it was more," Charlie mumbled, her cheeks suddenly warm. "You helped out a lot this year, Matt. I really appreciated it, even if I didn't say so sometimes."

"I know," he said, smiling. "Well, aren't you gonna open yours? Or are we gonna stand here till Foster gets his shotgun out and asks me my intentions?"

Charlie snickered at the unlikely picture. "Fat chance." Her fingers plucked at the awkwardly wrapped smallness of the package. "Is it—oh, Matt! They're gorgeous!"

The last glimmerings of sunset made the burnished gold hoops glimmer as she held them up. "Oh, wow," she said. "You shouldn't have. I mean, really—" She shook her head, knowing without seeing the inside of the jeweler's box that the earrings were solid gold.

"You like 'em?" She could barely make out his face in the twilight.

"Oh, yes, but—"

"You got pierced ears?"

"You know I do, but—"

"Then put 'em on, so I can see them on you."

"Well . . ." she smiled, capitulating. "Okay." Unerringly, her fingers found the small indentations and she slipped the gold hoops into place. "There. How do they look?"

Matt reached into the kitchen and flipped on the porch light. For a long second his dark eyes studied her, then he grinned and nodded. "Great. Just like I imagined."

"Thank you, Matt," she whispered, looking up at him. "They're really beautiful . . ." He seemed very tall in the dim porch light, very close. As their eyes met, he raised his hand as though to touch her face, then, instead, brushed her short hair back from her earlobes.

Charlie's gaze held his for a long moment, then she half-turned away. "We ought to go back in."

"Yeah," he said, moving past her to open the screen door.

"Matt, wait—" Charlie reached out to touch his arm almost before she realized what she was doing. As he turned back to her, she reached up hesitantly to cup his face with both hands, feeling the faint roughness of his day's growth of beard beneath her palms. Gently she tugged his head down, standing on tiptoe to kiss him gently on the mouth.

After a long second she drew away, then began to lower her hands. Matt reached up to encircle her wrists, stopping her. His hands were hard, calloused, strong and warm. "Hey," he whispered. "You didn't run."

"No," she said. Her heart was racing inside her chest, the way it had when she jumped Sylvester over that enormous ditch last week. Charlie could feel the warmth of his grip spread all through her, making her light-headed.

He was so close his breath touched her face, but he only stood there, holding her wrists, watching her intently. "Why didn't you run?"

"Because you didn't chase me," she answered frankly. "Anyone'll tell you the worst way to try catching a horse is to run after it."

He let go of her wrists as a slow grin spread over his face. "That go for mules, too?"

CHAPTER 13

Bluegrass or Bust?

Charlie, Tommy John, and Peter sat in a booth at Mando's Cafe on Highway 90 West, hunched over Cokes and dogeared issues of *Practical Horseman*. "Here," Peter said, reading slowly, syllable by syllable. "Lexington. Preliminary to Advanced Levels. Three-Day Event."

Tommy John's dark features wrinkled into a frown. "Where's Lexington?"

Peter looked up, his soft, perpetually puzzled brown eyes questioning. "KY?"

"Kentucky," Charlie supplied, impatiently. "Doggone it, aren't there any around here?"

Christmas had come and gone, and Charlie had finally confided the secret of her ambitions for Sylvester to her co-workers at the stockyards. At first they were skeptical, but after she sent the big gray soaring over a row of oil drums with brush piled on top, then made him "dance"—as Peter had put it—they agreed with her that the gelding had talent and potential beyond that of any of the other horses now in the stockyards.

Charlie had even dared to confide in them her ambition to take Sylvester to a Three-Day Event, hoping that if he won, he'd sell for so much money that Mrs. Daniels and the rest would have to concede forever that training horses could be a real job. And then if people began bringing their horses to her to train . . . Charlie had even envisioned herself one day with a neat little house, snug, well-kept stables, and beautiful, split-railed paddocks . . .

"Well, there's a jumping class this spring over at Fort Stockton, that's only about eighty miles from here," Tommy John said. "Of course, they probably show only hunter-style jumping. But it wouldn't hurt to just let him get used to the noise and the crowds."

"Right." Charlie nodded. "Good idea. Lenny over at Rancher's Feed and Supply told me they have dressage tests up in El Paso. That's not much further. If only I had a way to get him there!"

"I'll haul you, Charlie," Tommy John offered. "If you'll pay the gas. As long as Rosita doesn't mind."

"That's great, Tommy! Ask her, please."

"She probably won't mind—specially if she gets to come along. She can go shopping or to a movie if she gets bored at the show."

"And I'll come too, Charlie, to groom for you," Peter said. "You done good with that horse, and I love to see you dance like you did the other day."

She gave him a quick pat on the shoulder. "Thanks, Pete. You guys are great. Together we're gonna—"

A tall shadow loomed over the page in front of Charlie and she looked up to see Matt Grey. "Hi," he said, dragging up a chair and sitting down on it backwards, resting his folded arms on the chairback. "What's up?"

"Who asked you to sit down?" Charlie demanded, hoping he hadn't seen the opened magazines. Matt would give her a hard time about jumping Sylvester, she knew it instinctively. Heck, he worried every time she climbed on a bronc. And since Christmas, things had been so relaxed and pleasant between them that she didn't want to mess it up.

"I got a tow in the lot," he said, as if that explained everything. "Saw your truck out there."

"Here's a picture of that Lexington course, Charlie. Looks tough," Tommy John said, handing her the magazine.

Oh well, the cat's out of the bag now, she thought, taking the issue. "That's okay," she said, "Sylvester can . . ." Her eyes widened as she took in the height, breadth, and stomach-twisting dificulty of the obstacles. "Lordy!" she whistled softly. "*Look* at those jumps!"

It wasn't so much that the fences were so *high;* Sylvester had probably jumped higher out on the mesa over piles of deadwood stumps and sagebrush she'd dragged into place. But to clear these obstacles, the horse often had to jump from awkward positions, with only a few strides between fences. One of the jumps pictured was on top of a hillock. The horse had to leap *uphill,* over the fence, then continue without ever landing down over a six-foot bank. The dropoff was sheer and uncompromising—Charlie's stomach tightened as she tried to imagine hanging on over such a drop. And there was another jump where the horse had to jump down into belly-deep water, leaping through it, then taking off out of the water up yet another bank and fence!

The magazine was abruptly snatched from her fingers. "What are you looking at?" Matt demanded, staring at the article. His dark eyes studied the pictured obstacles for a long moment before he turned to Charlie. "You on drugs?"

"Does it say how to sign up?" Peter asked.

"If it's like Cutting Horse Trials," Tommy John offered, "she's got to do it early. Like right now."

"When is it?" Charlie asked.

"September," Tommy said. "You got less than nine months to train."

"How do I sign up? Do I have to pay money?" she asked.

"We can phone from Foster's office," Peter said. "Get 'em to send you the info and entry forms. He never checks the bill."

Tommy John gave him an admiring—albeit surprised—look. "When did you grow brains? That's a great idea."

Peter laughed, pleased.

"Oh, but—" Charlie had been studying the pictures again. "Look how much all this would cost, you guys. Look at the clothes you have to have. I'd have to have a new saddle . . . maybe more than one. Can't forget the dressage part. And then there's motels, and trailering . . ." She sighed.

"I got fifty bucks," Tommy John said. "I might as well blow it on a friend as blow it at pool."

"And I got twenty." Peter smiled. "It's all yours, Charlie. So you and Sylvester can go to Lexington and dance. Send me a postcard, willya?"

Her eyes stung as Charlie looked at them, shaking her head. "You crazy nuts. I'd need a lot more than that. But thanks."

"You know, that cop you sold the Appaloosa to was out the other day, bragging about how his boy likes Appy," Tommy John said. "He thinks you're 'bout as good as you think you are. And *he's* running the Police Charity this year."

Charlie grimaced. "I don't need charity."

Matt Grey stood up abruptly, angrily. "You need your head examined, that's what you need!" He walked out without looking back.

CHAPTER 14

In Training

"Jumps must be no less than twenty strides apart." Grant read aloud from a page of *Practical Horseman*. It was a chilly, bright winter day out in the back field behind the stockyards. The boy watched as Tommy John and Peter, grunting with exertion, carefully maneuvered a railroad tie into position atop a stack of old, heavily creosoted ties. The solid barrier was above belt-buckle height on Peter, the taller of the two men.

"There," Tommy John grunted, eyeing the obstacle with satisfaction. "He'll have to pick 'em up every time he goes over *that*."

"What were you saying?" Peter asked Grant, polishing his glasses, steamed up from sweat.

"I said that 'jumps must be no less than twenty strides apart.' " The boy looked puzzled. "Does that mean a horse's stride, or a person's?"

"Dunno," Peter said.

"Listen!" Grant looked up. "This part's *important.*" He began reading again. "The Event course generally includes a water jump, a coffin, a Helsinki and an Irish bank."

They all looked at each other blankly. Finally Tommy John moved over to peer down at the page along with the boy. "Are those the pictures of 'em?"

Charlie was happy. She had her job back, she and the boys were snug and reasonably comfortable out in John Foster's barn, and she was able to ride Sylvester every day weather permitted. She was working on conditioning as well as training the gelding, following the advice in an article in *Practical Horseman.* Every four days, she'd trot Sylvester for five minutes at a time, resting for two minutes between each trotting interval, and repeating the trotting and resting cycle three times.

After three weeks of trotting up and down hills, Sylvester was ready to begin cantering during the intervals. Tomorrow she'd start with three minutes of slow cantering, gradually working up to hand-galloping for seven minutes, then resting for three, during the required three intervals.

Charlie now followed a regular Eventing training schedule. Conditioning intervals one day, dressage the next, jumping and trail riding the third, dressage on the fourth, then start all over again. She loved it, and the big gelding seemed to, also. When Charlie whistled for him each afternoon when she got off work, she found him waiting for her at the gate to his pen in the stockyards.

The one fly in Charlene Railsberg's ointment was Matt Grey's absence. He hadn't come over or called since that day in the cafe when he'd told her she was crazy, and even when she drove over to pick up Grant after an afternoon's work at Webb's, Matt remained in his office or under the vehicle he was fixing. Charlie missed him more than she was willing to admit to herself.

She was thinking about Matt one Sunday in late February while riding home from her afternoon workout, only to flush hotly when she realized the idle tune she'd been humming as Sylvester ambled along was "Love's Been a Little Bit Hard on Me." *If he can't understand that you're entitled to have ambitions and dreams,* she told herself fiercely, *then he's not someone worth feeling sorry over!* Her angry thoughts were distracted by Seth, astride his new friend, Gladys, as he came galloping toward her, waving and shouting.

"What is it?" she yelled, afraid something had happened to Grant or John Foster.

"Charlie!" the little boy yelled, clinging hard to the white mule's stubby mane, "It's ready! It's ready!"

"What's ready?"

"The jumping course for Sylvester! Peter and Tommy John finished the last fence just a little while ago! They said you can look at it now!"

"Yeeehah!" Charlie sent the big horse into a pounding gallop, bending low over his mane. They thundered down the side of the dirt road, then around the barn and out back, followed by Seth and Gladys, who were rapidly left behind.

Peter was sitting on a log in the late afternoon sun, while Tommy John squatted on his heels, smoking. Grant sat beside them, still poring over the Combined Training Rule Book. Charlie looked past them to the back fields.

The acres had been transformed from rolling prairie to a

cross-country course . . . Even if it didn't look like any cross-country course she'd ever seen pictured in *Practical Horseman*.

An ancient wagonbed was festooned with an equally ancient white bedspread to form a spread jump. Tires were strung on a cable, with a ditch dug in front of them. A picnic table and chairs formed an oxer. Tommy John and Peter had sunk posts and built a section of post-and-rail extending vertically up a nearby hill so the height of the jump varied with the steepness of the hillside. She saw a spidery crisscross of piled rails. Huge piles of logs and brush draped with tattered shower curtains . . . and more.

"Lordy, Lordy," Charlie said, open-mouthed. "I don't know what to say, guys. You worked your tails off!"

Tommy John smiled. "It isn't the same as the Lexington course, Charlie, but the heights on the tallest parts of the solid obstacles are all at least three foot seven inches—the same as what you'll have to jump in Kentucky. Some of 'em are higher."

He pointed across the course to a box-like structure piled to overflowing with juniper and sagebrush until it resembled a gray-green wall. "The brush ones are between four-and-a-half and five foot. Of course, you don't have to jump *them* as clean 'cause they ain't gonna hurt his legs if he touches 'em."

Peter patted the big gray's neck and Sylvester amiably slobbered on his jacket sleeve. "We dug all the old junk out of the barns to build 'em, Charlie. We figured that if you can get him to jump these weird-lookin' things, he ought to be willing to tackle anything he sees."

"I can never thank you for all this," she said, looking

down at them. "I . . . thanks, anything I can ever do . . . pay you back—"

"Don't get all gushy, Charlie," Peter said, obviously pleased by her reaction. "We started it on lunch hours and today's Sunday. Our own time."

"Now you be careful," Tommy John said, holding up a warning hand. "When the book said 'solid' we built 'em so these suckers *are*. We tied 'em together with rope on the tops, but even so, if he hits one square, both of you'll be lucky to walk away sound. So pick up your feet, okay?"

"Okay," she said. "Think I'll try a couple of the smaller ones now, before sunset."

"There's only one thing missing that you'll have to take at Lexington, Charlie," Grant said. "A water jump, usually accompanied by a drop down into the water, and a jump out. There's not enough water in this part of the country to build one. I don't know what you're gonna find to practice on."

"I'll think of something," she said, turning Sylvester toward the first of the brush jumps. The gelding was quivering with excitement and eagerness. "Now just settle down . . . settle down . . ." She trotted the horse toward the jump, then let his strides lengthen into a long-striding canter.

The brush loomed ahead, looking even more formidable now that she was in front of it. Charlie forced herself to study it objectively, sizing up Sylvester's probable take-off point. Usually Sylvester liked to jump big, but with a spread brush like this one, he couldn't jump too far back, or he might catch his hind legs in it.

That's it . . . here we go . . . Sylvester, slightly suspicious of this new obstacle, stood far back from it, springing upward with a savage leap that nearly unseated his rider. Charlie clamped her knees into the worn old flat saddle, barely managing to let her hands move forward to follow the motion of the gelding's head. For a long second they soared like two creatures who had a choice whether or not to come back to earth, then Sylvester's body was arching down, and Charlie sat back in the saddle, bracing herself against the shock of the horse's forefeet striking the ground.

They were down. Sylvester snorted excitedly, but calmed after a second. She turned him, heading back toward the others. "Hey, that looked great!" Tommy John shouted.

"Cleared it by a mile!" Grant yelled.

"Charlie, you were flyin'!" Peter exclaimed.

"Yeah, I nearly flew right off," she grimaced. "I didn't expect him to jump so early or so big, and I got left behind when he took off. I just barely avoided yanking the reins and hitting him in the mouth with the bit."

"You'll learn, Charlie," Peter said, his eyes shining. "I know you can do it."

"Are you kidding?" Matt Grey glanced skeptically at Grant Railsberg as they stood looking out over the cross-country course behind the stockyards. "She actually gets Sylvester to *jump* all these things?"

"Clean as a whistle, most of the time." The younger boy nodded proudly. "She's gonna try and take him to Burleson next month in April if Tommy John can trailer her. They've got a horse trials there, and she's got to enter two of them before she can ride at Lexington."

"Is she still set on that?"

"You know my sister."

"Yeah," Matt said ruefully. "Guess that shouldn't surprise me none. Trailering to Burleson . . ." he calculated roughly in his head, "that's 500 miles or more. She and Tommy John would have to take at least one day off, even if they drove all night. And where's she gonna get the clothes, and the money?"

"She called over to Sul Ross and found a girl in the horse club over there who's her size. When she told this girl Nancy about what she was trying to do, Nancy told her that since she doesn't have time to show now that she's in college, she'd loan her clothes and tack to Charlie for the two Texas trials."

"But that horse has never even been at any kind of a showgrounds—except for a rodeo. He'll probably buck rather than jump."

"Charlie doesn't think so. She took him over to a dressage test up in El Paso last weekend. They held it in a big indoor arena."

"She win?"

"No, she got a 51 score."

"Is that good or bad?"

"Pretty average for a first time, I think. Me and Seth went along to watch. At least the crowds and loudspeakers don't seem to bother Sylvester."

"What do they do? Was it fun to watch?"

"Watching dressage is like watching cement set. Not exciting like the jumping, but Charlie says it's really harder in most ways."

Matt glanced around. "Will she be jumping out here today?"

"It's the right day for it. She usually rides up to the

mesa and back to warm up first.'' The younger boy's glance was sharp and knowing. ''Planning on sticking around?''

Matt shrugged. ''Been awhile since I've seen her. Guess I might as well.''

Grant smiled. ''Right. Well, she ought to be—'' he squinted into the lowering sun. ''Here she comes.''

The gray horse trotted out from the opposite side of the auction barn toward the cross-country course. Charlie didn't notice the two watchers as she let Sylvester lengthen his strides to a ground-eating hand gallop. Matt squinted, turning his head to follow the swiftly moving gelding with Charlie's slight form balanced lightly over the animal's withers. ''She's heading for that big solid one!'' he said, in alarm.

''Yeah, the railroad ties,'' Grant said. ''She takes a different route most times around, so he won't get too used to jumping any set pattern.''

Matt held his breath as the big gray thundered up to the massive obstacle, rose into the air, and came down with scarcely a break in stride. ''She did it!'' he breathed.

'' 'Course she did,'' Grant said. ''Just watch.''

Nervously, Matt did so as the pair continued around the course. Some of the angles at which Charlie attempted the obstacles had him sweating—several times he was sure Sylvester couldn't possibly have enough distance for a successful takeoff. But each time, over the twenty or so jumps on the course, the gray took off and soared over the jumps. Finally Charlie turned and came back toward them, still sitting forward in her saddle, in jumping position.

''What's she doing now?'' Grant sounded puzzled. ''She's finished the course—''

''She's heading for the water tank!'' Matt exclaimed.

The cement tank sat at the corner of the stockyards fence. It was no more than two-and-a-half feet high, but it was at least eight feet in diameter. "Charlie!" Matt shouted, beginning to run toward it, "No!"

Sylvester headed for the tank at a headlong gallop, with Charlie urging him on. Matt could almost see a diabolical gleam in the gray gelding's eye as the horse gathered himself as though to jump—and then, as Charlie moved farther forward, giving him his head for the takeoff, he stopped dead, popping his shoulder forward as he turned slightly away from the tank.

Charlie flew over Sylvester's head like Peter Pan, to land square in the center of the water with a gigantic splash.

"You crazy kid!" Matt heard John Foster's voice behind him. The old man was cussing like a trooper as he passed Matt at a dead run. Charlie scrambled up sputtering and spitting, only to have Foster yank her one-handed out of the water tank. "You stupid idiot! You forgot your helmet! Don't *ever* jump without a helmet again! You came within an inch of splitting your pea-brained head open like a melon!"

Charlie wiped her eyes with her sopping sleeve and looked up at the old man. "But I've got a trial coming up and no water jump. How do I get him to jump water?"

"Not by killing yourself, Charlie! Now get your horse and walk him before he colics from standing hot!"

Foster let her go and strode away, seething.

"*I'll* walk the horse, Charlie," Grant said. "You get into some dry clothes. It's chilly out here."

"Thanks, Grant," Charlie said. "I'll be out to untack him in a minute."

Matt and Charlie started back to the barn. Seeing her shiver, he took off his leather jacket and draped it over her shoulders. Charlie barely noticed. "That old creep," she mumbled. "Sylvester loves to jump, he's a natural at it. It was *my* fault he refused. I didn't keep enough leg on him. I didn't ride him right."

"Appeared to me like he didn't like the water," Matt observed. "He had kind of a look in his eye coming up on it."

"But he'll have to jump water at the Talland II at Burleson, and again in Waco! What am I gonna do?"

"You need Foster on your side," Matt said.

"Why?" She glared at him. "I'm doing okay without him."

"You're doing great," he said. "Much as I hate to admit I was wrong, you looked like that's what you were born to do. I never saw a horse jump like that before, Charlie. You've done a great job training him. But Foster could—"

"I've got to change," she said, stopping inside the barn. "Can we talk about this later?"

"Sure," he said. "As long as you don't mind talking about it."

"*You* were the one giving *me* the cold shoulder for the past two months," she reminded him, with a wry smile.

"All right," he said. "Rub it in all you want. I'll pick you up at eight, and we'll go for a ride and talk, okay?"

"Okay."

Charlie scrambled into the cab of Matt's pickup. "Where are we going?" she asked, as he pulled out of Foster's yard.

"East on Highway 90," he said. "Thought we'd drive out to the Marfa Air Field and watch the ghost lights."

Charlie glared at him indignantly. "Listen to me, Matthew Grey, if you think that I'm so glad to finally see you that I'm gonna agree to parking all night with you, *you're* the one needs your head examined! Foster's gonna put the boys to bed, but I've gotta be home—"

"Stow it," Matt said brusquely, driving. "If I were lusting that bad over your skinny bones, there's plenty of deserted spots between here and the Air Field, Charlie. I said 'talk' and I meant it. Besides, I never take a girl parking the same place the other guys do . . . I got a better place, one Stanley Marsh never cruises."

She was startled. "You do? Why—" she began, then abruptly shut her mouth and sat back in the seat.

Matt chuckled. "Why haven't I ever taken you up there? Why, Charlie, honey, I have too much respect for you . . . and for those hard little knuckles of yours. I saw the mouse you gave George Rhoades—it was a beaut."

"Matt Grey—" she tried to stay mad, but finally gave in and began to laugh. "You're impossible!"

"So my mom tells me all the time."

Charlie leaned her head back against the seat and watched Highway 90 slip by. It was nice to be out on this brisk night, traveling fast, with no place specific to go. It made her feel free, for the first time in a long time.

Finally Matt turned the pickup into the old entrance to the Marfa Air Field. He pulled up, set the parking brake, then they both looked south.

"There they are," Matt said, after a few minutes.

Against the dark mountainside several miles away, a blue light flickered, then split into two separate lights that waved and danced for many moments before finally winking out. Another, whiter light began, then more lights followed, flicking on and off like stars, or sometimes like campfires.

"What do *you* think they are, Matt?" Charlie asked.

He stretched his long legs and leaned back in the seat deliberately. "I don't worry about what they are, and frankly, I hope nobody ever finds out. The Marfa ghost lights are one of those mysteries that ought to *stay* a mystery. Like the Loch Ness monster, or Bigfoot."

"How long have people been seeing them?"

"As long as anyone was around to report it. There's an old legend that they're search fires kindled by the ghost of an old Apache Indian chief who got separated from his people, and still roams the mountain looking for them. They say he lights campfires, hoping it will help him find his lost ones."

Charlie shuddered. "That's such a lonely idea."

"It's more romantic than swamp gas, or moonlight on an undiscovered mica vein."

They sat in silence for several minutes, watching one spectacular display of a brilliant sapphire colored light that split and separated five times.

Finally Charlie stirred. "Well, if we're gonna talk, I guess we'd better do it. Why do you think John Foster could help me, even if I could talk him into it?"

"Well, you know he was in the cavalry. He fought the Japanese on horseback, in Indochina."

"So?"

"So the cavalry *invented* Three-Day horse trials. Foster was telling me about it one night at Quanch's. They used to call the event 'The Military' in the Olympics. You've always said Foster knows more about horses than anyone you ever met."

Charlie thought about it. "I don't know. I wanted to do it all myself. I figured that way nobody could say I wasn't a real horse trainer."

"Hey, you've done more so far than anyone could have guessed. But even if Sylvester is some kind of equine Rocky Balboa, you're gonna need coaching. Even Rocky had Mickey, remember?"

"Yeah," she admitted slowly. "You might be right. It would be a good idea to have someone coaching me . . . especially in dressage. You can't see yourself ride . . ."

"Right. It was Foster, after all, who taught you how to ride in the first place. I know he wants you to succeed."

"Then why hasn't he helped me?"

Matt turned to face her. "Why haven't you asked him?"

Matt turned the pickup back into the driveway. "I've got to check on the boys," Charlie said. "They ought to be asleep by now."

He stood outside waiting for her, enjoying the early spring breeze, looking up at the brilliant stars. This far away from any city, they seemed heartbreakingly close, and Matt remembered vividly one night when he was a little younger than Seth . . . he'd climbed the Chinese elm outside his window and, standing on the topmost swaying branch, knapsack over his shoulder, he'd reached up to grab a handful of those "diamonds in the sky" . . .

Matt smiled ruefully, rubbing the old knot on his collarbone, shaking his head. Kids had the craziest dreams. He'd been lucky that when he fell all he'd broken was his clavicle—it could well have been his neck. The experience had taught him caution against reaching too high, even at that early age.

Caution. . . . He'd always played it safe. After two years at Sul Ross, he'd dropped out when his father died, to run the gas station that had belonged to his uncle. There hadn't been anyone else to take care of his mother, and she'd never worked. Even though she'd told him she'd get a job, encouraged him to get his degree, to see how far he could go playing football . . . Matt had decided his responsibility lay at home.

It had been nearly a year since he'd made that decision, and he still wondered sometimes if he'd done the right thing . . .

"They're fine," Charlie said, startling him out of his reverie. "Sound asleep. Seth has his He-Man and the Dragonwalker in bed with him."

Matt smiled at her. "Guess he really likes it. I'm glad."

"Let's go beard the lion in his den," Charlie said. "I hope he hasn't been drinking."

John Foster *had* been drinking; Matt could tell as soon as he saw the old man that he was far, far gone. He sighed, reaching for Charlie's arm to suggest they wait until another time, but he was too late. She walked over to stand directly in Foster's line-of-sight. "I'm sorry, Mr. Foster."

Red-rimmed blue eyes focused blurrily as the man looked up at her. "Sorry?" he mumbled, slurring the word almost past understanding, "I'm sorry too. Your mother was th' sweetest woman ever walked this earth . . . 'n I—"

"I'm sorry that I jumped Sylvester wrong today, Mr. Foster. I'm apologizing."

"She was a pretty woman, sure . . . but her *beauty*—"

Foster belched, "her beauty came from th' inside . . . she glowed like a . . ." he cast about for words, "like a lightbulb when she came inna room . . ."

Matt stepped forward. "John, listen. Charlie's trying to—"

"I'd like you to help me," Charlie broke in. "With training Sylvester. I *know* he can be a winner. Then you can sell him for a *lot* of money."

Foster shook his finger at her, not listening. "*Told* Lena to leave that sonofa—"

"I want to train horses, Mr. Foster," Charlie broke in, a desperate edge to her voice, "but nobody thinks that's a real job. If I can take Sylvester to Lexington and win—"

The old man ignored her. "Your Daddy knew every two-bit oilfield floozy in Midland, and he—"

"*John, shut up!*" Matt snapped, seeing Charlie's expression.

The old man subsided a little, giving her a guilty look, but still not ready to abandon his tirade. "Lena deserved better, thass all 'm sayin'."

Charlie's eyes were bright with tears, and her voice shook slightly. "She told me that you taught a horse to dance. I was eight years old, and I've never forgotten her face when she told me about watching you ride. She told me she saw you, and your horse was dancing in the moonlight."

She swallowed hard. "And when she told me that, I thought, 'I'm gonna do that. Someday I'm gonna learn to teach horses to dance.' "

Foster sloshed a little more whiskey into his glass. "Your daddy was so diseased he'd infect a woman just looking at her. When I think about him *touching* her—"

he pounded his fist jarringly against the tabletop, sending his glass toppling over.

"When she talked about you," Charlie grabbed his arm, her voice low, intense, "magic would fill up that crummy little trailer. Magic would drown out the yelling and the hitting and the whiskey." She snatched up Foster's bottle suddenly, strode over to the sink and poured it out. The old man made a motion to go after her, but was unable to stand.

"Yeah, magic," Charlie whispered. "The magic of a horse dancing in the moonlight. Is there anything left of that magic in you, Mr. Foster? Can you teach me how to do it? Will you help me?"

The old man turned away from her, peering up at Matt. "He was drunk when he drove them into Sibilo Creek, you know that?"

Matt put a protective arm around Charlie as she walked back to stand beside him. "Everyone knows that, John."

"I was crazy 'bout that woman . . ."

"Everyone knows that, too," Matt said.

"You had a funny way of showing it!" Charlie's shoulders were shaking beneath Matt's arm. "You can go straight to Hades, Mr. Foster!"

Glaring at the old man, she pulled away from Matt, then the screen door slammed back on its hinges and she bolted out.

"You did it this time, John," Matt said, giving Foster a hard look before he followed her.

Charlie was already across the yard, running down the road past the barn. Matt raced after her, gaining because of his longer legs, but having to work at it. He was panting by the time he caught her, near the old windmill. ''Charlie! Wait up!''

He grabbed her arm, and she whirled on him. ''I don't need that old creep!''

Matt struggled to control his breathing. ''Okay. Okay. But just because Foster won't help you, doesn't mean I won't.''

She stared at him. The moon had risen by this time, and he could see her incredulous expression. After a moment, her eyes narrowed suspiciously, and she said, ''Yeah? For how much of my body?''

Matt laughed, pulling her to him, holding her in a brief, hard hug. ''For whatever's left—after you've finished killing yourself.''

She stared at him in the moonlight for a long moment. Finally she grinned and stuck out her hand. ''Deal.''

Solemnly, they shook.

CHAPTER 15

Faith, Hope, and Police Charity

Charlie came home from the Burleson Horse Trial in April tired and discouraged—but not ready to give up. Sylvester had improved his dressage performance slightly, but he'd refused the cross-country water jump the first time, receiving a twenty-point penalty. Charlie had gotten him over it by prompt use of her whip, but knew now that her experience with Foster's water tank was no fluke; Sylvester didn't like water, and had no intention of jumping it without protest.

In addition to the twenty penalty points, his refusal caused Sylvester to complete the course late, thus earning him an additional seven penalty points for exceeding the Optimum Time.

The stadium jumping portion of the horse trial also proved a disappointment when Sylvester, used to skimming closely over cross-country brushes, jumped the post-and-rail studded with fake brush on the top so close he knocked the topmost brush off. That meant another five penalty points.

At the end of the day, when she collected her score sheet from a steward, Charlie stood trying to puzzle it out for nearly a minute. The number "80.2" was circled. "Is this my score?" she asked the man.

"Yes," he said, pointing to the number. "The lower the overall score in Eventing, the better. Forty, for example, is an excellent score."

"Oh," Charlie said, looking despondently at the score-sheet. "I see."

"Is this your first competition?" the man asked.

"Yes."

"Well, that's not a bad score for your first time out, young lady. Don't be discouraged."

"Really?" Charlie smiled, feeling her spirits lift a trifle. "Thank you very much!"

But on the way home, dozing restlessly on Matt's shoulder as he drove Tommy John's rig with Sylvester munching hay in the ancient stock trailer, she relived her debacle at the water jump over and over. *How am I going to get him to jump the water?* was the question that never left her.

She refused to look at the even bigger problem that stood in the way of her ambition to go to Lexington: lack of money. The two trips to Horse Trials in Texas were going to use up most of the money she'd managed to save over the winter . . .

Two nights later, Matt came over for supper. Charlie dished up the meal (stew, made from vegetables and three quail Grant had bagged) and for many moments after Charlie asked the blessing, there was no sound except that of hungry people eating. Finally Charlie, with a glance at Matt, ventured, "I want to move Sylvester up to the barn here at the house, Mr. Foster. That way I can ride both mornings and evenings as the light gets longer. Matt's gonna help me lay out a dressage ring, and we're gonna build some stadium-type jumps.''

Foster didn't look at her as he took another bite, chewing vigorously. He swallowed, then deliberately buttered a biscuit.

Charlie glanced at Matt again, who nodded encouragingly. ''There was an Olympic training and conditioning schedule in your *Practical Horseman*, Mr. Foster, and I've been following it. But I really need somebody to coach me . . .'' She looked straight at him. ''I'd like *you* to coach me . . .''

Foster took another biscuit. ''Well, I won't.''

Matt spoke up. ''We want to go to Kentucky, John. There's a Three-Day Event in September, in Lexington. Charlie's done a tremendous job training Sylvester.''

''She's not going,'' the old man said, glaring at them.

''Yes, I am,'' Charlie said. ''If I have to buy Sylvester from you myself and work a year to pay for it, I'm getting there somehow.''

He sighed. ''You don't understand, Charlie! They go off the sides of cliffs! They jump fences built in the middle of rivers. It's too dangerous. I won't let you go.''

''I've already been to one,'' she said. ''Talland II Horse Trials, up in Burleson. I know what they jump.''

'' 'Zat where you two went?'' The old man looked faintly surprised. ''I thought you were gone up to El Paso again, or to Fort Stockton.''

''You didn't ask, so we didn't say,'' Matt said. ''Charlie did okay for a first time.''

''Yeah? What'd you score?''

Charlie pushed stew across her plate. "80.2 overall."

The old man's eyebrows went up a fraction. "Huh. Not good enough to do anything in Kentucky, honey. Not by a long shot. Did he take the water?"

"After a refusal," she admitted.

"See? And a real Three-Day Event is bound to be tougher than those Horse Trials."

"The Olympic team paid a quarter of a million dollars for a horse last year, somebody told me at Burleson—"

Foster slammed his hand on the table, making the glasses dance. "Would you *forget* this stuff about the Olympic team? They've got horses coming out their ears. They sure as sh—" he looked at Grant and Seth, and made a swift alteration in context, "—shooting don't need a bucking horse from Marfa, Texas!" He scooped up another mouthful of stew and jammed it into his mouth, chewing fiercely. "Maybe," he swallowed, "maybe I'll take you to Colorado to a Young Riders competition, Charlie. Next spring. Maybe."

He glared at Matt. "And don't you go building her any jumps."

The silence was broken many minutes later when Grant announced, "This is quail. Nobody noticed."

"I noticed," Seth said. "It's great."

"It's not cooked right," Foster grumbled. "Quail are supposed to be split and broiled like chicken."

"I *like* it this way!" Seth defended his brother and sister.

"If you want it cooked different, Mr. Foster," Charlie said evenly, but with an underlying edge, "*you* cook it."

The old man laughed angrily. "Now here's your mule talking, Matt. All she rides and talks is Olympic, all she cooks is stew. Heaven help you if you get hitched to this jenny! She'll—''

Charlie got up and walked out, slamming the door.

John Foster turned to Matt. ''Matt—''

''Oh, no, John,'' the younger man shook his head. ''I'm not going after her this time. You did it, you can fix it. If she'll even listen to you. If I was her, I'd have decked you.''

Grumbling, Foster wiped his mouth and got up.

He found Charlie in the barn, sitting on some hay bales near Gladys's stall, the cat Pearl in her lap. She stroked it as he came in, turning on the light near the beds, and did not look up.

Foster felt himself getting angry all over again. ''Now look here, Charlie. If you can't take a joke, you can't ride my horse, you can't work for me, and you can't live on my property! If there's one thing I can't stand, it's—''

She interrupted him as though she hadn't been listening. ''Next time you dump on Grant, we're moving out.''

''I didn't dump on Grant!''

''You know how hard it is for a ten-year-old to shoot a quail?''

''So move out! You'd be doing me a favor!''

She glared at him, furious. ''You bitch about your lousy kids who never amounted to anything. Did you ever stop to think—''

''What do my kids have to do with anything?'' he roared.

''Did you make them that way, Mr. Foster? Did you dump on everything they wanted to do? Everything they did? Did you tell them it was dangerous, that they weren't good enough—that it wasn't cooked right?'' Her eyes were bright with anger even in the dimness of the barn. ''Did you kill them, Mr. Foster? Like you're killing me?''

He took a step back as she finished softly, ''Like you killed my mother?''

Silence.

Finally Foster found his voice, heard it harsh and yet querulous at the same time. ''You have no idea what you're talking about.''

''Yes I do.'' She looked up at him, her mouth hard and thin. ''She'd have left Daddy if she'd had a place to go, somebody to protect her. Somebody strong enough to stand by her, take her away from here. If you'd opened your door, let her know you'd take her—and us, she'd never have left us—she'd have gone. You know that as much as I do.''

John Foster swallowed, shaken. ''What you're suggesting is not true, Charlie. It's absolutely not true. Lena and I never—''

''Oh, I know you two never did anything,'' she said bitterly. ''Mama would've, 'cause she really loved you. But you held it against her that she married Daddy when you were gone. No matter what Preacher Ahrens says, I kept wishin' she *had* gone to you. She might've sinned, but at least she'd still be alive.''

Foster sat down on a bale of hay opposite her, the pain inside him threatening to rise up and overwhelm him. Charlie was right, he'd always known it . . . tears threatened somewhere behind his eyes, but he fought them back.

She picked the cat up in her arms, stroking her. Pearl's purr was a rasping buzz in the stillness. ''She needed you. Now I need you. And you're gonna let it all go by this time, too.''

She stopped at the doorway, her voice hard and uncompromising. "No wonder you drink, Mr. Foster. You keep letting people down."

Stanley Marsh looked out the window of John Foster's office at the stockyards. "There she is, now. I'll have to go by and thank her."

"Thank her for what?" Foster asked, lighting his pipe.

"For the look in Tim's eyes yesterday when he won that Championship belt buckle at the rodeo over in Fort Stockton. There were kids there sixteen, seventeen years old, some of 'em riding twenty thousand dollar Quarter horses. And he whipped them!"

Foster looked outside, saw dust blowing around in the parking lot. "Shaping up to be a nasty one," he commented, seeing Charlie on Sylvester working stock.

"That makes the third trophy this year for Tim," Marsh said. "Here, John, I want you to give Charlie this." He handed the man a check.

Foster took it, saw it was made out to Charlene Railsberg, for one hundred dollars! "What's this for?" he asked gruffly.

"A bonus, for training Appy," Marsh said, still grinning. "That gal earned it. I'd have paid twice that much for the look on my kid's face yesterday."

"I gave Charlie five hundred out of the thousand I sold Appy to you for, Stan," Foster protested. "You don't have to—"

"I know I don't," Marsh said. "No arguments, John. That little gal earned this."

"She's got the touch, all right," Foster said reluctantly,

folding the check and putting it in his pocket. "I'll be sure to give her this. She could probably use it to go to Waco in three weeks."

"She'll need more than that to get to Kentucky," Marsh observed.

Foster's face tightened with anger. "*Kentucky,*" he said, making the word sound like an obscenity. "That's all I hear."

Marsh laughed. "She came to the police station last week, you know? Talked to the thick-skinned cynic who runs the Police Charity. Me."

Foster wheeled on him. "Stanley, you didn't—" he strode over to the window, flung it up. "*Charlie!* Get your butt up—" He squinted out into the gathering dust. "Blast!" he said. "Nobody's ever where I want 'em!"

"We've never given it to an individual," Marsh continued mildly, as though Foster hadn't spoken. "Usually we use the money to buy something for the hospital."

"Well, you're not gonna start changing that now," Foster said ominously.

"I know her chances aren't good," Marsh began, "but—"

Just then the door slammed back on its hinges as Charlie burst into the room, windblown, her neckerchief pulled down from her mouth and nose to leave the lower half of her face clean. Dust puffed out of the creases of her shirt and jeans. "Mr. Foster, there's a guy leaving us some real sick cattle!"

"Can't *anyone* ever come into this office and just sit down like a normal human being?" Foster yelled, flapping his arms in exasperation.

Charlie ignored the outburst in her excitement. "This sucker's unloading Mississips with sores on their backs, huge open gross bleeding sores! You can see *maggots* in them, Mr. Foster, practically waving their arms around in there! It's awful, they'll contaminate our stock! The smell is so bad you'd gag!"

Foster was already out the door. Charlie raced after him, with Marsh puffing along behind.

Foster reached the stock truck, squinting against the swirling dust, finally seeing the driver, a huge, burly man with tattooed forearms who leaned against the door with a clipboard in his hand. The back gates to the truck were already closed.

"Hey," Foster shouted over the rising roar of the wind, "you can't unload those cattle here! Those animals are infected!"

The man shrugged, narrow-eyed against the dust. "I just did, buddy."

"Well, we're going to undo it for you," Foster snapped, nodding to Peter and Charlie, mounted and waiting.

Kerchiefs pulled over their mouths and noses against the stench and dust, the two wranglers quickly herded the pitiful cattle back into the loading chute. Foster moved over and opened the stock truck's gates.

"Wait a minute!" the driver shouted, "who do you think you are?"

"I'm the owner!" Foster shouted. "Those steers need medical attention. They can't be sold for human consumption like that; it's illegal! You broke the law just bringing 'em across the State line!"

"But I got a bill here to pick up a load of sheep!" the

driver said, cursing as the cows thudded back up the ramp and Foster closed the doors. The big man grabbed the stockyards owner by the arm, his fist clenching. "I'm gonna—"

Stanley Marsh hove into view, and the sight of the uniform made the trucker hesitate. "Well, I declare!" Marsh said, shielding his eyes from the dust, "what a smell! I'd say John's right, that those cattle have been transported illegally!" Reaching past the trucker, he jerked open the cab door and climbed into the truck.

After a second he leaned back out into the whipping wind and dust, holding his uniform cap on his head with one hand. "Just as I suspected," he said holding up a sheaf of papers, "you're out of date and overdue on every license you got here, boy. And I think I'm gonna go call on my radio for a Health Inspector to pick you up and look over them cows." Marsh swung out of the truck, heading for the man.

Cursing, the trucker spun on his heel and raced away, jumped up into the cab on the driver's side, then started the engine, pulling out of the yard with a clashing of gears, heading for highway 67 East. Marsh walked over to his police cruiser, climbed in to use his radio.

Foster looked over at Charlie and Peter, who had leaned over in their saddles to shake hands with each other. "Well, well," he smiled reluctantly, "we're easily pleased with ourselves today, aren't we?"

"That oughta fix that sucker," Marsh said, rejoining them. "The Health Inspector'll have his hide as soon as they catch up to him. Which won't take long. Can't drive fast in this."

"Guess we'd better get these horses in before the storm gets worse," Charlie said, turning Sylvester back into the wide aisle of the auction barn.

"Charlie," Captain Marsh called.

"Yessir?" she turned back.

"We voted to give you the money."

"You *did*?" Even under the masking kerchief Foster could see her face split in a delighted grin. "*Yeeeeeehahhh!*" she whooped, and Sylvester, thinking it was rodeo time all over again, went bucking down the aisle.

Stanley Marsh began to laugh, until he saw Foster's stormy expression. "Now look here, John. That kid's been kicked around since the day she was born. Her daddy was the sorriest sonofagun ever puked up my jail. You gave her a hand, gave her a job, gave her a sense of worth training your horses, and gave all three of 'em a place to live—"

"So I'm running for God," Foster snarled, "what's that got to do with you handing her money?"

"Why, John," Marsh's jowly face creased into a beatific smile, "we just want in on the act!"

Two weeks later, Charlene Railsberg went on the shopping trip of her dreams. First she went to see her friend Sandy Martin, who had set up a tailor and dressmaking shop in her home. Sandy, following patterns ordered from equestrian catalogs, had sewn most of the three different outfits Charlie would need for each phase of the Three-Day Event at Lexington.

With Sandy looking on, Charlie slipped into the tight white britches with the suede pads sewn to the insides of the knees to help her grip, and the yellow-and-black striped Eventing shirt. "I feel like a bumblebee," she mumbled, looking down at herself. "Black and yellow stripes!"

"I made you two pairs of the show britches," Sandy said, "in case you have a fall and one gets dirty. And here are the ones you can wear for practice. They're black, so they won't show dirt."

Charlie turned slowly in front of the mirror, sucking in her stomach, gazing skeptically at the skintight britches. Her red and black bikini panties were clearly visible through the knit material. "Wow," Charlie mumbled. "These pants show everything! I've gotta ride in front of strangers dressed like *this?*" She poked at her hipbones.

"You better wear white undies," Sandy advised matter-of-factly. Charlie looked over at her, and after a second both of them began to giggle.

"And here are the other things," Sandy said. "I haven't finished them, yet. A double-breasted black three-button coat with tails for the dressage, which you'll wear with a white shirt, a canary yellow vest, and a stock for a tie. You're gonna have to practice tying the stock around your neck. They give instructions in the pattern."

"Wow," Charlie mumbled, "when I wore Nancy's clothes she had one of those ready-tied ones."

"Well, you want to do it right, don't you?"

"Sure," Charlie said. "What else is there?"

"Well, here's your white shirt and the black riding coat for the stadium jumping. You wear your stock for that, or you could wear a tie if you wanted. Here's the gold safety pin you'll need to fasten the stock."

"Lordy!" Charlie shook her head. "I never had these

many clothes to my name before. And to think I managed to ride all these years in just my jeans and cowboy boots. It's a wonder I stayed on."

Sandy grinned at the sarcasm. "Rules are rules, Charlie. Just be sure you don't grab the wrong coat the wrong day, okay?"

"Okay." She smiled.

Charlie's next stop was Perry's Western Wear, run by a paunchy disagreeable man named F.G. (neither Charlie nor anyone else in Marfa knew what the initials stood for). He settled a tophat on Charlie's head, and they both stood looking at the picture she made, wearing her beat-up Acme boots, University of Texas tee-shirt, and—the tophat. "You sure this is right?" Charlie asked skeptically, eyeing herself in the mirror.

"I called Miller's in New York City," he said. "Ain't no mistake. You could get a hunt cap, but they recommended this to go with the jacket I described you wuz wearin' for that dress . . . dress—"

"Dressage," she put in mechanically. "Well, I guess I'll have to wear it around the house so I get used to it. Do I look silly?"

He ignored her. "Now this is the Caliente helmet for the jumping part and the cross-country." Charlie nodded, then dug in her bag for the black-and-yellow striped cover, pulling it over the black nylon cover already on the helmet. "It fits," she said, putting the tophat on the counter and trying on the Caliente, fastening the padded chin strap.

"Black and yellow?" F.G. asked skeptically. "High school colors?"

Charlie grinned. "I'm a public works project. Like the Marfa water tank."

Even F.G. had to smile.

Her next stop was the boot store. Sam Ewing, a heavy-set black man, carefully lifted down a tall pair of black dressage boots, cut higher on the outside of the leg than on the inside. Charlie stroked the shining black leather. "Oh, they're beautiful," she murmured. "Just beautiful."

"You better try 'em on, honey," Sammy said. "Make sure they fit."

She sat down on a rickety chair, drew the boots on over her knee socks and britches. "Like a glove," she said, smiling, wriggling her toes inside the boots, enjoying the smell of new leather. "Like they were made just for me."

Sammy spat tobacco. "Which they was, honey. First custom-made English style boots I ever made, and I'm right proud of 'em."

"You should be. Thanks, Sammy!"

"The best for the best. You go back East to Kentucky and knock 'em dead, honey. You an' that Sylvester Stallone horse of yours."

Charlie's last stop was Rancher's Feed and Tack, owned and managed by Lenny Simmons, a slender, balding man in his early fifties. Lenny had managed a tack store in Maryland before moving to Texas for the dry climate and the water (Marfa didn't need to chlorinate its water; it ran naturally pure). When she came into the store, he nodded. "Got it all right here, special rush order." He began piling tack and equipment in front of Charlie, rattling off the name of each item as he laid it down:

"Here's your leather dressage girth, then your elastic webbed girth for cross-country. Then here's the overgirth, that's for cross country, too, you fasten it *over* your saddle for extra security. Here are two fleece saddle pads. The brown is for practice, the white is for showing. This is a coolout sheet to put over him while he's being walked. Here's a blanket, for trailering and if it's cold. Make sure he doesn't sweat underneath it. Here are the Hampa boots to protect his legs while he's jumping. Here's your dressage saddle, it's a Passier. This is your Eventing saddle, for jumping, it's a Giddens . . ." Charlie could hardly see over the pile by now, and still Lenny kept adding to it!

". . . Here's the breastplate to anchor the saddle, then the running martingale attachment for it you'll use during the jumping and cross-country. *Don't* forget to use *only* the breastplate during the dressage. Martingales are forbidden there. Here's the bridle. You said you want to keep him from opening his mouth or slipping his tongue over the bit, so I ordered a 'flash' or 'Mexican' noseband. It won't cut off his wind like a dropped noseband."

"Lordy!" Charlie muttered. Even Lenny could barely see over the pile by now.

"Here's your first aid kit, track bandages, tail wrap, and braiding bands. A spare bit, cheek piece, and rubber reins for the cross-country, so your hands won't slip. This box has got screw-on studs for the bottom of his shoes, for traction during the cross-country. Get your farrier to drill the holes for 'em. Here are your stirrups and irons. I put those non-skid rubber pieces on 'em so your feet won't slip. New halter, leadshank, fly spray, whip, and blunt spurs. *And* your wrist stopwatch. That's it."

Lenny was completely hidden behind the wall of horse supplies. "Wow," Charlie said weakly. "I don't even know what some of that stuff is *for*."

"I thought you were supposed to know what you're doing," he chided.

"Well, I thought I did, but I had no idea all these things are considered everyday equipment for Eventing."

"Well, they are, at the Preliminary level. Did you bring your truck? I'll help you carry it out."

As they walked out, staggering under the load, Charlie asked, "Have you ever been to one of these shows, Lenny, when you lived back East?"

"Remember, it's not called a show, Charlie. It's a Trial, or an Event."

"Right. But have you?"

"Years ago. I saw the U.S. Equestrian Team win the 1976 Olympics in Canada."

"I'm gonna be riding tonight, after I get off work," she said. "Will you come out and tell me if I've put it all on right, and if I'm doing anything really stupid?"

"Well . . . all right," Lenny agreed.

Matt Grey drove up to the stockyards and parked. He noticed that two other trucks and a Volkswagen Jetta sat on the lot, which was odd, since the yard had been closed for about half an hour. He got out and walked around the auction barn, heading for the back fields and Charlie's cross-country course.

When he reached the back, he found Sammy Ewing, F.G. Perry, and Lenny Simmons sitting on the fence with Grant, Tommy John, and Peter, while Seth sat nearby, high up on Gladys so he could see. Charlie was moving Sylvester at an extended trot, the horse's strides long, balanced and beautifully sweeping, while his head and body remained "on the bit."

Matt stopped a little behind Charlie's audience, wondering what the men were doing there. "Hi, Matt," a voice said, and turning, he saw Stanley Marsh behind him. "Want a beer?"

"Thanks," he said, accepting a Coors. "What's going on?"

"Charlie went shopping today, and I guess everyone wanted to see their stuff in use. I came over to watch her do the cross-country course."

As they talked, John Foster came out of the auction barn, shaking his head no at Marsh's offer of a beer. They stood watching as Charlie cantered over to the fence. "Doesn't he look great in all his new gear?" she asked, cheeks pink with excitement.

Everyone agreed that Sylvester looked wonderful in his new finery. "They want to see him jump, Charlie," Grant said. "Take him around. And be sure you try the new water jump we dug."

"Water?" rumbled Sammy. "If you get water on that new leather, Charlie, make sure you dry it good, or the thread'll rot."

"Okay," she agreed, taking the Caliente helmet Grant held out to her and snapping the chin strap. Then she shortened her stirrup leathers to jumping length, and turned the big gelding back toward the course. "C'mon, Sylvester, let's show 'em how we'll do it in Lexington."

Matt, Stanley Marsh and John Foster stood watching as she eased the gelding into a hand-gallop, leaning forward in her saddle. Sylvester flew over the post-and-rails, the railroad ties, the Helsinki on the hill, the coffin with its combination of a post-and-rail, ditch, then another post-

and-rail, then the gray leaped to the top of the four-foot bank and off it, flew over the brush jumps, the wagonbed, and all the rest of the cross-country jumps.

Sammy, Stanley Marsh, Matt, F.G., and Lenny all clapped for each successfully negotiated obstacle. Foster stood in glowering silence.

As Charlie swung by on her last lap, she slowed Sylvester for a breather, and the newcomers stepped forward to pat him and congratulate her on her performance. Matt and Foster were left standing together behind the fence. "A star is born," Matt commented, watching with a wry smile.

"Yeah," Foster said sourly.

"John, the tighter I tried to hang onto her, the more she fought to get away," Matt said with a sigh. "So I let go, but I may have lost her anyway—before I ever had her."

"Wait'll *she* loses," Foster said.

Matt looked at him.

"She doesn't have a chance, Matt!" Foster said, shaking his head. "She's gonna come apart."

"You that sure she's gonna lose?"

"Against Olympic-caliber riders?" He gave the younger man an eloquent look. "Sure, I'm sure."

"Maybe she wouldn't lose, if you'd coach her."

"It wouldn't do any good," Foster mumbled.

"Is that it?" Matt grabbed the old man's arm, his dark eyes intent. "Or is it that you're not really afraid *she'll* come apart, it's that you can't face the fear that *you* might. Too much of a risk, right, John? It's easier to let her get whipped all by herself, than for you to stick out your neck—and your reputation—for her, isn't it?"

"You—" the old man glared at him.

Matt was already striding away.

"Hey, Charlie!" Grant called. "Do the water, now!"

"Okay," she agreed reluctantly, turning Sylvester toward the new water jump with the low post-and-rails in front of it.

Sylvester gathered speed, and Charlie let him see that she was carrying her whip. The gelding's ears flickered back and forth, and Charlie could feel his uncertainty. She wished Grant hadn't mentioned the new water jump—she'd wanted to school over it privately, hoping that she could get Sylvester to jump it by herself a couple of times before trying to show off. But she couldn't resist the challenge.

"C'mon," she whispered to the horse, urging him on with legs and seat. "C'mon!"

Sylvester bunched his muscles, pushed with his hindquarters, and then—

—stopped dead, ducking his head. Charlie felt her body flung forward despite her efforts to grip with her legs, to grab mane—

—then she was flying through the air, to hit the water and the mud beneath with a resounding splash. Wind knocked out, Charlie flailed helplessly, trying to gasp, but it was a panicky second before she could get any air back into her lungs. Her head swam as she inhaled, then she struggled to her feet, seeing Sylvester standing nearby, a mischievous gleam in his dark eyes. "You!" she sloshed toward the horse, "I oughta beat your silly head in for that!"

"Take it easy, Charlie." A hand caught her elbow, helping her out of the water. "He's still got a lot to learn—and so do you."

She looked up at John Foster's blue eyes, seeing the faint crinkles around them as he smiled.

"Who's gonna teach us?" she gasped, feeling an irrational hope at the look on his face.

"Guess I am. Everyone else in Marfa is helping, so I guess I can't not do my part," he said. "You better get a good night's sleep, honey—we got a lot of work in front of us, starting tomorrow."

Muddy and wet as she was, Charlie flung her arms around the old man, planting a brown kiss on his cheek. "I'll work!" she promised. "We can do it!"

CHAPTER 16

Trial by Water

‘‘No, no, *no!* You’re not going *forward*, Charlie, you’re just going sideways! In a half-pass you’ve got to have *impulsion*, the horse has got to go *forward* as well as sideways! You’re letting him die on you!’’ John Foster’s voice was a graveled shout in the darkening twilight. The low white railing marking the far end of the square dressage arena in the pasture outside Foster’s house was lost in shadows. Foster stood in the pool of brilliant glare cast by the security light on the barn, watching, frowning.

‘‘Stop a second and come here,’’ the old man commanded, and Charlie rode over on Sylvester. ‘‘Now, listen to me. You’ve taught him wrong. You’ve got him doing more of a Western horse’s sidepass than a dressage horse’s half-pass. With the half-pass, he’s got to impulse and move *forward, never* lose that forward motion, even when your legs and hands tell him to begin his sideways motion. Understand?’’

"How do I do that?"

"More leg, Charlie! Outside leg slightly behind the girth, inside leg on the girth, and his head cocked just a *tiny* bit in the direction you're going. You ought to just be able to see the shine of his inside eye."

"It's so dark I can barely see anything," she grumbled.

"Well, it's not Sylvester that's screwing up here, Charlie, it's *you,* and we're staying out here till you get it right!"

"Okay," she said, picking up her reins and straightening her shoulders.

The old man watched as she collected the gelding at the walk, nodding. "Now put him in a trot! Good! Shorten your reins a hair! Good! Now think *forward!* Think it with your whole body! Good! Now begin your half-pass! Leg, *leg,* LEG!"

Charlie trotted on around the corner until she reached Foster, then sat waiting tensely. "That was better," the old man said mildly.

"Thank you, God," Charlie said, looking up at the early stars. "My legs feel like they're gonna fall off."

"Practice it tomorrow morning, and I'll check you again tomorrow evening. Remember, only four days to Waco."

"I know," she sighed, throwing a leg over Sylvester's neck and sliding down, feeling her leg muscles ache as she landed. And she'd thought she'd worked hard before! Foster was a tartar, demanding perfection in the tiniest of details. She and Sylvester had had several hard days since he'd begun coaching them.

Leading the horse, reins slack, she began walking the gelding to cool him off, grateful at least that she no longer had to ride him back to the stockyards, since Sylvester now shared the barn with her and the boys—and Gladys, of course.

As she walked, her thoughts went back to the first morning she and Foster had gone out together, the old man on his mare, Penny, and Charlie riding Sylvester . . .

They'd ridden past the mesa to a small lake several miles from the stockyards. It was fed by a narrow, swift-running creek that had been dammed partway to form the lake.

"All right now," Foster had indicated the stream, swift and shallow, its rocky bed clearly visible, "ride him through that."

"He'll go," she half-protested, and Sylvester, after a hard look at the water, went. "He'll *cross* water, he just doesn't want anything to do with jumping into it."

"We'll do this for a couple of days at least, just let you ride back and forth across different locations along this creek. Main reason why horses don't like jumping into water is that they can't see the bottom if the water's deep enough. So we'll teach him confidence this way, starting out shallow enough so he can see the bottom, then working into crossing deeper and deeper places, faster and faster. When he'll canter across without any fuss, then we'll try jumping. Just a little rail, at first, then a real jump. That's it. Let him take it at his own speed at first. Now again."

"But I've got to jump water in Waco!"

"Got to build up his confidence, Charlie. He's got to know that you wouldn't ask him to jump into anything that's gonna hurt him. That takes practice and work."

"Did the cavalry really fight the Japanese on horseback,

Mr. Foster?'' she had asked, trotting through the creek for the sixth time.

''Yeah,'' he'd said. ''Nine hundred of us. Two thousand horses. We'd gallop at a tank, Charlie, four of us, each from a different direction . . . each with a grenade. When we ran out of grenades, we made Molotov cocktails by putting gasoline in soda pop bottles. I was young and dumb enough to think it was fun.''

''Matt said you stopped 'em.''

''So they say.'' The old man leaned off Penny to spit tobacco at a yucca plant. ''In the end there were only a hundred of us left. The last order we got through was to slaughter the horses for food.''

''Did you?'' Charlie had given him a sideways look as Sylvester plunged into the stream, throwing up crystalline shimmers of water.

''Most of 'em.'' His bushy white brows drew forward in a frown. ''All right, now, you've let your seat go! You're gonna have to jump him through this eventually, so let's see some leg and seat! Don't turn those toes out! Leg, *leg*—''

Sylvester snorted in the darkness, and Charlie came back to the present with a start. Rubbing his neck and feeling his chest, she realized the horse was dry and breathing normally, ready to be put up.

Leading him into the barn, she unsaddled him, put on his halter, and snapped on the crossties. After brushing Sylvester thoroughly, Charlie checked his legs, rubbing them down with a brace of equal parts water and liniment. Then she examined his back and belly for any lumps or swellings. There were none, so she put him in the stall, then fed him. Sylvester was a fairly calm-dispositioned horse, an ''easy keeper,'' but since she'd begun conditioning him, she'd ended up feeding him nearly twice what he'd eaten before the hard work began. Leaving him to munch contentedly, Charlie picked up her tack and started wearily back to the house. Time to start supper—but she was so tired she only wanted to lie down and sleep.

''Hi, sis!'' Appetizing odors drifted out of the screen door on the warm spring breeze. Grant stood at the stove, busily stirring something, while Seth set the table. ''We knew you'd be tired, so we got dinner.''

Charlie smiled at them. ''You're the best brothers anyone ever had, guys. I'm gonna take a shower.''

''Leave your tack here, Charlie,'' Matt offered, from across the room. ''I'll clean it.''

''Thanks,'' she said. ''This is really turning into a team effort, isn't it?''

''Nope, I'm just sticking around to protect my investment.'' He grinned. ''Stan Marsh hit me up for a tenner for the Police Charity, long before we knew most of it'd be going to Lexington with you.''

''I'm not thinking about Lexington,'' she said, turning back from the bathroom door. ''One thing at a time. Right now all I'm concentrating on is the Trial at Waco. If I don't get around the cross-country course with no disobediences or falls, I don't qualify for Lexington.''

''Think positive,'' Matt said.

She nodded grimly. ''I can't afford not to.''

Waco. The Cedarwood Spring Horse Trials. It was hard to believe she was really here, finally, on the cross-country course.

The water jump next . . . the water jump next . . . the

words drummed over and over in Charlie's mind, in rhythm to Sylvester's galloping hooves as they raced over the tough brownish prairie grass. This time it wasn't a dream, or an imagined fantasy; she was *here,* at Waco, and the water jump was next!

Charlie concentrated on not tensing up, not betraying any of the anxiety she felt hovering at the back of her mind to Sylvester. They were following the hoofmarks along an open field, toward a slope downhill marking the stream where the water jump combination was located.

Red flag on right . . . white on left . . . she reminded herself, as Sylvester swooped over the edge of the hillside. Charlie steadied his head, keeping plenty of leg on him, resisting the urge to sit back. It was hard to stay forward while galloping downhill, hard not to sit back on the horse's loins. But the horse needed his hindquarters free so he could push off.

"C'mon, Sylvester!" she whispered fiercely into the back-tipped ear that was cocked back to hear her. "C'mon!" She kept her legs on him as he reached the bottom of the slope, urging him toward the first fence, a low post-and-rail. "C'mon!"

She felt the horse tense as he saw the water, muddy and churned by the hooves of the horses who had gone before. Charlie swung her whip an inch or so, reminding him that she was carrying it. *"Come on!"* she muttered, refusing to let him hesitate, riding him toward the obstacle as though she could pick him up bodily and propel him over it.

And Sylvester went. He jumped high, landing in the water with a huge splash, sending mud flying everywhere. A big clot of it plopped onto Charlie's cheek, but she couldn't spare a second to think about it; there was still the post-and-rails on the other side of the stream to jump.

Don't you dare stop now, Sylvester! she thought, sitting firm, squeezing the horse onward with her legs and seat. Two plunging, sloshing strides, and the gray gelding leaped uphill, out of the stream and over the rails, then they were galloping up the slope and away.

All right! Charlie thought, exhilarated. *Three cheers for John Foster!*

Charlie stood looking at the posted cross-country scoresheet, barely conscious of Matt dabbing mud off her cheek. "Time faults," she grumbled. "Four penalty points worth of time faults! I knew I should have let him go a little faster!"

"Forget that now," Foster snapped, resaddling Sylvester as Grant frantically brushed the mud off his legs. "You've got the stadium jumping to worry about now! Get changed!"

Charlie balanced precariously in the blanket-draped front of the horse trailer, pulling on her clean britches and shirt, brushing mechanically at her short hair. *No time for lipstick, I'm gonna look like a ghost . . .*

Careful where she put her feet on the trailer's floor, she quickly sponged off her muddy boots, then pulled them on. Grabbing her black riding coat, she resnapped her helmet, mounted, then turned Sylvester to line up for the stadium jumping.

Her round went fine until the gray, tired from the cross-country, pulled a rail down on the in-and-out. Charlie heard it fall behind her, but, obeying Foster's instructions to never look back, she kept going.

When her round was over, she went looking for the steward to get her scores.

Charlie felt her spirits lift when she saw a circled "59.9." At least she'd done better, at least Sylvester hadn't refused; at least she had qualified for Lex—

"Charlie!" Matt was shaking her arm, as she stood studying her scoresheet. "Didn't you hear your name called?"

"Huh?"

"You won sixth place! Go get your ribbon!"

Stunned, Charlie turned to mount and Matt boosted her back into the saddle. She rode into the awards ring, stood at the end of the line of sleek, shining horses, and finally was handed a green satin ribbon with a rosette at the top.

"Pretty good," Foster said, nodding at her as she rode out and slid off, while the boys exclaimed over the ribbon.

But not good enough, Charlie thought, *not good enough to win at Lexington.* She knew it without being told.

Three more months to go, she thought, on the way home, watching the white lines flash by on Route 84 West, Seth's sleeping body cuddled into the curve of her arm. She was tired, but sleep was a long way off. *Three months,* she thought. *That's not much time. We've still got a long way to go . . .*

Clip . . . clop . . . clip . . . clop. . . Charlie sat up in her sleeping bag in Foster's barn, hearing the distant sound of a horse walking on hard ground. The night July breeze was warm against her bare arms and legs.

A dream? she wondered fuzzily, but after a second, the sound came again, even more distant now.

Sylvester? she thought, her heart jolting against her ribs.

Gladys? Did someone get out? The wrangler's worst fear—loose stock—brought her upright. Quickly she pulled on her jeans, slipped her feet into sneakers, then dragged her sweatshirt over her tousled hair. Moving quietly to avoid disturbing her brothers, she tiptoed out into the night.

The full moon was well up. Checking her watch, she saw it was half-past midnight. Once outside, she could hear the hoofbeats again, more distinctly. They were coming from the dressage arena.

Charlie moved soft-footed, strangely reluctant to call out. There in the moonlight was Sylvester, the blue-white moonglow bleaching his coat to purest silver, to match the hair of the old man who rode him.

She peered from behind a Chinese elm to watch as Foster finished warming the horse up, then began schooling him. Sylvester moved with lightness and sureness, seemingly obeying commands as though they were his own idea, rather than his rider's.

The walk: steady, cadenced, each hoof placed distinctly and surely. The collected trot: slow, hesitating, balanced, then the extended trot, with its surge of power and elegance. The half-pass: Sylvester moved diagonally across the arena, his head cocked fractionally in the direction of his lateral movement, his body bent so his forelegs and hindlegs each traveled on a different track. With each stride, his outside fore and hind legs crossed over and in front of the inside legs. The movement was flawless, balanced, supple—a study in grace.

Then, the canter: collected, slow, majestic. Extended canter, strong, surging, yet still controlled. Lead changes: Sylvester skipped gracefully across the ring, for all the world like a little kid let out of school, joyful, ebullient.

And all the while the old man sat like a statue, scarcely moving. Even the creak of the saddle leather seemed muted. Charlie forgot to breathe, it was so beautiful.

So this is why Sylvester's been doing so much better lately, she thought. *Foster's been schooling him at night, sometimes!* Tears prickled behind her eyelids, thinking of how hard the old man had worked these last couple of months to coach her, how, gradually, the whiskey bottles and the nights at Quanch's had become a thing of the past. It had been weeks since he'd had even a beer.

He's done so much for me, she thought. *I have to win at Lexington . . . I can't let him down.*

Overcome by the beauty of the night, the moment, Charlie watched as, together, Sylvester and John Foster danced in the moonlight.

CHAPTER 17

Lexington at Last

John Foster flicked on the turn signal of his big, road-worn pickup, then made a right. "This is the place!" Charlie said excitedly, looking at the sign that read "Kentucky Horse Park." Below the sign was a poster proclaiming "Three Day Event—Novice, Preliminary, and Advanced Level, September 6, 7, 8."

Seth, who was perched on Charlie's lap, squirmed excitedly as the pickup rumbled up the winding drive lined on both sides with tall dark wooden fences. Beautiful slender-legged horses grazed in spacious pastures, and seemingly everywhere they looked there were huge trees and winding streams. "Wow," Seth said, for the fourth time that morning, "it sure looks *different* here. Green everywhere! And look at all the creeks!"

"Yeah," Matt said, craning his head past Grant, who sat on *his* lap. "Pretty country. Pretty *rich* country."

"I'll say," Charlie mumbled, glancing back at Foster's

ancient Stidham Quarter Horse trailer. Sylvester's pricked ears were barely visible over the metal front of the trailer—he was so tall in comparison to the quarter horses Foster usually hauled that they'd had to cut out the roof to keep him from banging his head. The dusty bed of the pickup was crammed with suitcases, tack, feed, hay and other equipment.

"Aren't we *ever* gonna reach the end of this road?" Seth squirmed again. "I have to go to the bathroom!"

"You can hang on a few more minutes," Charlie said. "How do you think I feel—you sitting on me for three days?"

"Hang on Seth, I think we're getting there," Foster said, as the truck rumbled over a stone-sided bridge. Below them they could see yet another good-sized stream. The pickup rattled up a hill, then, abruptly, the road turned left into a huge equestrian center, lined on all sides by stables, equipment sheds, and one massive low barn that enclosed a full-sized indoor riding arena.

Looking around them, they could see rolling hills that contained paddocks, several jumping rings, the dressage arena surrounded by spectator grandstands, the steeplechase track, and to the north, the cross-country course stretching seemingly into infinity.

Even Seth was beyond words.

The area around the barns was teeming with people in tweed hacking jackets, or expensive suits and dresses. Big goose-necked horse trailers were hooked to expensive pickup trucks, and some rigs were accompanied by campers painted in stable colors. Enormous horse vans overshadowed the trailers. Grooms walked horses in the sunshine to limber them up.

The parking lot on their right was filled with Mercedes, BMWs, even a Maserati, the first Charlie had ever seen. Foster drove the pickup into the trailer area, backing up expertly between two massive horse vans. Charlie hugged Seth suddenly, frightened. What was she, Charlene Railsberg from Marfa, Texas, doing here? Who was she kidding?

The pickup stopped, and Foster set the brake and turned off the ignition with a sigh.

"I'll go sign in and get her number and find out where she's supposed to go," Matt said, climbing out. He stretched until his joints cracked.

"I'll take Seth to find the bathroom," Charlie said, "if that's okay with you, Mr. Foster."

"Sure, Charlie," the old man said. "I'll get Sylvester out and start walking him. He's bound to be as stiff as we are after all that riding. When you get back, we'll take him over for his vet check. Have you got his Coggins Test?"

"Right here." Charlie held up a manila envelope. "The negative Coggins, along with his immunization and worming records. I wasn't sure what they'd want to see, so I brought them all."

"Okay, hang onto them," Foster said. "Matt, find out when the vets want to check him."

"Be right back," Matt said, and he and Grant started off.

"When the vets are done, you'd better tack him up and ride him for awhile to get the kinks out," Foster told Charlie. "Just a little walk, trot, and canter, nothing more, understand?"

"Right."

Charlie started across the yard, heading for the big barn, reasoning that rest room facilities were bound to be located in there. She felt stiff, gritty and tense, suddenly conscious of her down-at-the-heels Acme boots, faded jeans, and worn Western-yoke shirt. Defiantly, she tugged her battered Stetson down over her eyes, as she walked past a group of girls about her own age, all wearing tailored britches, custom-made boots, and elegant silk shirts.

As she passed them she heard somebody snicker, then the whole group laughed. "Cowboys . . ." she heard someone say, then another giggling murmur, ". . . make way for the hicks . . ."

Lips tight, feeling her cheeks burn, Charlie steered the tired little boy into the barn, refusing to give them the satisfaction of looking back. At the moment, though, she wanted nothing more than to turn around and head home for Marfa . . .

"Number 77," Grant said, admiring the number disk that would fasten to Sylvester's headstall, and the number vest Charlie would wear during the cross-country sequence. "That's a lucky number, Charlie."

"I sure hope so," she said. "I checked the location of the scoreboards. They're over near the dressage ring. I found Sylvester's and my name printed right there, near the bottom. I borrowed a pen and wrote 'For Sale' beside Sylvester's name."

"Have a soda," Foster said, handing her a Coke. "How'd he work?"

"Pretty good," she said. "I'm gonna have to walk the course this afternoon, when one of the officials is gonna take us around, and I'll get another chance tomorrow morning, before the dressage."

"Try and get around it three times if you can," Foster advised.

"My aching feet!" She grimaced. "That course is three and a quarter miles long!"

"Also," Foster cautioned, "don't forget to walk the steeplechase track. That's a shorter run, only about a mile and a half, and eight jumps, but you've got to *move* on it—24 miles per hour to avoid time penalties, and Sylvester isn't Man O'War, unfortunately. Those Thoroughbreds are gonna have the speed advantage in the steeplechase portion of the cross-country."

"He can move," Charlie said confidently. "And all the jumps are brush, I checked already."

"Yeah, but don't forget those brush fences have solid rails beneath the brush, and that they're all between four feet and four-foot-seven. And you have to jump them *fast*—there's no room for mistakes. So you walk that course, Charlie, understand?"

"Yessir."

"I'll walk both of 'em with you early tomorrow morning, when nobody's around, and we'll map out your strategy. We'll make notes and study 'em, try to visualize any problems ahead of time. That's half the trick, to *plan* your ride ahead of time. Design your ride to capitalize on your horse's strengths, and minimize his weaknesses. Got it?"

"Yessir."

"Sylvester all settled in his stall?"

"Yeah," Matt said. "Happy as a pig in a wallow, eating hay. Nothing temperamental about him."

"Good, that's the way we want him. Charlie, did you groom him good?"

"Yup. And I pulled his tail and wrapped it, so it'll lay

smooth. But he'll need a bath. He's got manure stains on his legs and flanks.'' Charlie took a bite out of a peanut butter and jelly sandwich left over from the stack she'd made to bring along on the trip. She made a face; the bread was stale, and the jelly had soaked through, but she kept eating. She was too hungry to be fussy, and there was still a lot to do before they could eat dinner and drive back to the motel.

''He'll get a bath tomorrow morning,'' Foster said. ''We've got time before the dressage.''

''Don't forget that I'll have to braid him,'' she reminded her coach.

''We'll wash his mane first,'' Foster said. ''Braiding a mane's easier when it's wet, anyway.''

The old man turned to Matt and the boys. ''Did you get all the stuff out of the truck and move it into the stall next to Sylvester? We have the use of it for our tack and feed.''

''All done,'' Matt reassured him. ''We even put up the folding chair so Charlie can sit down if she gets tired.''

''Trust me, she won't have much time to sit down,'' Foster said. ''Dressage day tomorrow won't be so bad, but the Endurance Test on the second day's gonna be hell on wheels. Remember, she's got a lot more to do at a Three-Day Event than just the cross-country part she did at those Horse Trials.''

''What else does she have to do?'' Seth asked. ''Will Sylvester get tired?''

''Real tired, Seth. First she's got to trot or slow canter during Phase A, Roads and Tracks, for three miles, then she goes to Phase B, the Steeplechase, for one and a half miles at a fast gallop, over jumps. Phase C is Roads and Tracks again for another three miles. Then she gets a ten-minute break before starting the cross-country course, which is a little over three miles and twenty-five or so jumps.''

Seth turned to his sister. ''You're gonna be busy, Charlie.''

She nodded. ''We sure are, Seth. I hope Sylvester and I hold up.''

''Sylvester's in rock-hard condition,'' Foster said. ''He's as fit as he's gonna get. Don't worry too much about him. Just worry about *you,* Charlie.''

She nodded, thinking that *that,* at least, wouldn't be hard. Worrying was something she was getting only too good at . . .

When the Event Official announced the escorted walk around the course, Charlie joined the group of riders and trainers. Foster, Matt and the boys had gone to the motel to register and unpack, and would return to pick her up in time for dinner.

Hovering on the fringes of the crowd of young riders, most of them male, she wished fervently that she'd brought at least a blouse or sweater to wear instead of her faded plaid Western shirt, with the sleeves rolled up to hide the ragged cuffs.

The other competitors, male and female alike, wore designer slacks, rugby shirts or cotton blouses, and carried jackets or Shetland sweaters. Charlie noticed one young woman about her own age, with dark curly hair and gamine features. Another young man was about Matt's age, wearing a zippered sweat jacket with ''USA'' lettered across the back.

The attractive dark-haired girl—Charlie heard her addressed as "Ariane"—was accompanied by a British trainer. Charlie edged as close as she dared, to listen to the advice he was giving his rider, as they stood looking at the combination making up obstacle number three, an "option fence"—which meant that the three closely spaced post-and-rails could each be approached from several different angles, according to how the rider placed his or her horse during the sequence of jumps.

"Foxfield doesn't mind jumping wide, Ariane," the trainer was saying, indicating the first post-and-rail, "but you'd be wise to take this first fence head-on. That'll put you at a slight angle when jumping the second post-and-rail, but that disadvantage is more than outweighed by the favorable shot you'll then have in getting over the corner post-and-rail, here. Come in at the wrong angle, and you'll wind up jumping a very wide spread indeed, and this fence is already formidable enough. Understand?"

Ariane nodded. Charlie studied the three fences, the last one actually comprised of two fences joining at the corner to form a spread, and tried to imagine herself two days from now riding at those big, solid jumps. Fear niggled in the back of her mind, and she fought it down, carefully noting the approximate height, footing, distance between fences, and width of the corner spread in her little notebook.

The group moved on around the course, and Charlie continued to trail Ariane and her trainer, making notes about everything she saw and heard. The Englishman was obviously an expert at Eventing strategy.

"Now this is the eleventh jump," he was saying, as they approached it. "The Lexington bank. Quite a challenge here, Ariane, quite a challenge."

Charlie looked at the nightmarish combination wide-eyed. "Challenge" was putting it mildly indeed! The jump started with a four-foot leap up onto a high, wide bank, then the horse had to cross the bank, then leap down two terraced drops where the total drop was nearly as high as Charlie's head.

Landing after the drop, the horse then had a bare two strides to gallop before the "bounce." The "bounce" consisted of two post-and-rail fences placed so close together that the horse, to negotiate them, must jump the first, then immediately upon landing, without taking a stride, take off to jump the second.

Charlie stood on the top of the Lexington bank looking down at the terraced drop, seeing that there wasn't space for the horse to land on the narrow ledge, but that he'd have to leap outward as well as down to avoid catching his legs. She slipped carefully over the drop herself, skidding down on the seat of her pants, only to slip off the ledge and nearly fall. A hand caught her arm, steadying her, and looking up, she saw it was the good-looking young rider in the "USA" jacket.

"Thanks," she said, brushing dirt off the seat of her jeans.

"My pleasure," he said, with a charming smile. He had light brown hair and vivid blue eyes. "I haven't seen you on the circuit before, have I?"

"No, this is my first," Charlie replied, studying the "bounce," scribbling a note about the footing in her notebook.

"Are you sure you're with the right group?" he asked, betraying surprise but managing not to seem condescending. "This is Prelim."

"I'm riding Prelim," Charlie told him, stretching her

legs to keep up with the group as they headed for the water jump.

"In your first season?" The young man hurried to stay beside her. "You must have bought a good, seasoned horse."

She shook her head. "No, it's his first season, too."

He gave her a long look as they strode across the thick green turf. "What's your name? I'll tell the ambulance crew to keep a special eye on you."

Charlie laughed, feeling her nervousness dissolve a little. "I'm Charlene, Charlene Railsberg. People call me Charlie."

"I'm Harris Pell, Charlie."

He offered his hand as they walked, and she shook it. Despite his elegant clothes and good looks, his palms were nearly as hard and calloused as her own, a horseman's hands. His fingers grasped hers for a second or two longer than mere politeness demanded. *What a flirt,* she thought. *He's nice, but I'd never trust him to take me to watch the ghost lights.*

"Harris, like the tweed?" she asked, giving him a quick sideways glance.

"People don't mention that," he said, mock-warningly.

"Oh? Where'd you get that jacket, Tweedy?" She grinned at him.

He laughed. "It's the team jacket."

"The Tweedy Team?"

"No, the U.S. Olympic Team."

"Are you kidding?" She stopped dead to look at him. "Lordy!"

He laughed again. "Where are you from? You've got the cutest accent."

Charlie hadn't ever thought about having any kind of accent, and felt a little self-conscious. "Texas."

"Really? Ever ride any broncs?"

"Lots."

"Tell me about them . . ."

"Score for number 117, Foxfield, owned by Mrs. Whitney Hyde of Lexington, Kentucky, and ridden by Ariane DeVogue, 71.4," the announcer's loudspeaker boomed.

Huh, thought Charlie, settling her top hat more firmly on her head, then checking her black leather gloves, *Sylvester did better than that in the dressage part of the Waco test. Of course, each set of judges scores differently . . .*

"Do I look okay?" she asked Matt, who was giving her boots a last rub with a rag.

"Great," he said, giving her a thumbs-up. "You'll knock 'em dead."

"I *feel* like an idiot. I'll never get used to riding in clothes this fancy," she mumbled, making sure that the bottom corners of her yellow vest just showed below the edge of her black tailed coat. Grant ran his grooming cloth one final time over Sylvester's black-and-white flecked neck, careful not to disarrange the meticulous braids Charlie had worked so hard on that morning.

"Guess I'd better start," she muttered, seeing an official point to her and nod. "I must be next." She handed Matt her long dressage whip and glanced down at her small blunt spurs to make sure they were correctly fastened.

"Good luck, Charlie!" they called as she started toward the entrance to the dressage arena, staying alert to make sure she didn't cross the path of any of the competitors who were warming up. Some riders, she'd found, didn't bother to look where they were going.

"Number 77 will be next," the loudspeaker said. Charlie's chest tightened, and for a horrible moment, the test movements that she'd so laboriously memorized vanished in a wave of fear. Then she forced herself to take one deep breath, then another. And another. *First you trot in, halt and salute at center point X,* she thought. *One thing at a time, take it easy . . .*

All the while she had been automatically riding Sylvester toward the entry gate. Her face felt frozen. *Take it easy,* she told herself. *It's just another test . . .*

"Entering the ring now, number 77, Charlene Railsberg riding Sylvester Stallone."

Charlie trotted Sylvester strongly into the arena, heading for the imaginary center point. When she reached it, she tightened her fingers on the reins and her seat in the saddle, bringing Sylvester to a stop. She was careful to keep her weight balanced evenly so the gelding would halt squarely, with all four feet evenly beneath him. *Good halt,* she thought mechanically, taking the reins in her left hand, then dropping her right hand down to her side as she inclined her head to the judges in the formal salute.

Now she was ready to start the test. *What do I do first?* she wondered, and the answer came to her. *Working trot from X to C, and turn left.*

Charlie tightened her leg muscles against Sylvester's barrel, and the gelding obediently trotted down the arena toward the judges standing just behind the C marker. She kept her hands light on the reins, pushing the horse forward with her seat slightly.

The working trot, properly executed, was supposed to

be a strong trot, but not particularly collected, and the horse was not required to extend much. As she reached the C marker, Charlie closed her fingers tightly on the left rein, squeezing her left leg against Sylvester's side, and he turned left.

Careful, she thought, concentrating totally, her body feeling as though it had grown roots into Sylvester's back, *not too fast . . . where do I go now? Oh, yes, continue working trot to E marker, then make a ten-meter circle.*

She continued around the arena, using her left leg and a slight tightening of the right rein to push Sylvester up into his corner. He was a very long-backed horse, and they'd always had trouble with corners. *I could have done that better,* she thought, *he can bend better than that.*

Then, almost before she knew where she was, she was around the corner and coming up fast on the E marker, halfway down the side of the square arena. *My first ten-meter circle,* she thought, judging the ground to plan the circumference. *Right here!*

Using her right leg and left hand, she guided the gelding into the circle. He went willingly, but he was circling to his left, his stiff side, and Charlie had to keep squeezing with her right leg behind the girth to make him bend his body along the curve.

As she finished the circle she saw, out of the corner of her eye, Foster, Matt, and the boys sitting in the front row of the grandstand, watching her tensely.

With an effort she wrenched her attention back to the test. *Now where?* she thought. *Working trot around to F marker, then shoulder-in from F down the straightaway to M,* her memory supplied.

The shoulder-in went well, as Sylvester was bending to

his right, his more supple side. *Now working trot from M to H, diagonal across to F, then another shoulder-in from K to H*. The second shoulder-in, with Sylvester being asked to bend to his left, was not as successful. Midway down the stretch, the gray gelding began to lose impulsion. Charlie sat down hard in the saddle, her outside leg squeezing and releasing behind the girth, her inside leg squeezing on the girth. In her mind, she could hear Foster shouting *Leg,* **Leg, LEG!**

Finally she was down the straightaway, and could let Sylvester relax a little into the working walk from H to M marker. At the M marker she picked up the working trot again, preparing for her other ten-meter circle at B marker. This one was to the right, and Sylvester bent nicely. Charlie realized suddenly that she was smiling, enjoying what she was doing.

As she finished the circle, she signaled Sylvester for a working canter, and he responded promptly. The rocking-chair motion was easier to sit than the trot, but it was harder work to keep Sylvester impulsing forward without going too fast. When Charlie reached K marker, she tightened the reins fractionally, sitting down hard, and Sylvester dropped to a trot. *Extended trot diagonally across the arena to M marker,* she reminded herself. *Push him on! Push!*

She was breathing hard by the time they reached M, but felt encouraged by the admiring smiles and nods of the watching crowd. *Don't get cocky, Charlene!* she admonished herself.

What next? Oh, Lord, the half-pass!

She dropped down to a working trot until she reached the H marker, then gave the signal—outside leg behind the girth, inside on the girth, shifting her weight fractionally to the inside, and closing her inside fingers slightly. *Please, Lord, don't let me mess up now!*

Sylvester was half-passing to his left, his worst side, but he was doing marvelously! Charlie heard a surprised, admiring murmur run through the crowd.

Then the half-pass was over, she was at F marker, and they could continue at the working trot to C marker. *Now the halt for five seconds at C.* Sylvester bobbled just a bit in his transition to the halt, but stopped squarely. *One thousand one, one thousand two—*

Charlie counted seconds in her mind, feeling Sylvester shift his weight uneasily, but he didn't—*Thank you, God!* —move his feet.

The test was now more than half through, and Charlie knew she was doing well. She smiled again. *What next? Oh, yes, working trot from C to B, then working canter to K, followed by extended canter across to M . . .*

After her final salute, Charlie walked out on a loose rein, patting Sylvester, smiling broadly, and heard a sudden commotion from the stands, accompanied by loud clapping. "All *right!*" "Way to go, Charlie!"

Looking over at her cheering section, she blew Foster, Matt, Seth and Grant a kiss.

"Some ride," said a male voice, and, turning, she saw Harris Pell sitting on a tall, elegant bay horse beside her. "Was he trained dressage?"

Charlie slid off. "He was trained to buck," she said. "That's a beautiful horse. Is he yours?"

"Yes, this is Betamax," he said. "A Swedish warmblood."

"Is it your ride now?"

"I'm watching for the signal."

"I'd like to see your test," she said, loosening her girth and running up her stirrup irons. "Will they let me walk him here?"

"Sure."

"We have a score for a previous contestant," the announcer said, suddenly. "In the Preliminary Division, for Number 77, Sylvester Stallone, owned by John Foster, ridden by Charlene Railsberg, the score is 68."

"All right!" Harris said. "You beat Ariane . . . she's going to be jealous, you know."

"Will she?" Charlie began walking Sylvester in a circle to cool him out.

"Sure." Harris let Betamax amble along beside her. "You have a gorgeous seat, Charlie."

She gave him a mock-exasperated look. "*You* have a dirty mouth, Tweedy."

"She did it!" Matt Grey said exuberantly, as he, John Foster, and the boys made their way through the crowd. "You have to admit, John, that was a beautiful test! She—" his words trailed off as he saw Charlie walking beside the young man in the red U.S. Olympic team coat. His face darkened, and he made a move forward, but was stopped by Foster's hand on his arm.

"She's selling the horse, son," the old man said.

"She's selling something, all right," Matt said bitterly, "but it's not the horse."

"The saddle?" Seth inquired.

Matt cleared his throat, conscious of Foster's amused glance. "Never mind, Seth."

CHAPTER 18

Complications and Confidences

"Now listen here, Charlie, if you don't want to fall off that horse tomorrow during the cross-country, you've gotta eat." John Foster picked up a yellow styrofoam container and shoved it at Charlie. "Here, if the hamburgers are too greasy, try the chicken nuggets. Get something in your stomach, and that's an order!"

Charlie looked at him rebelliously. The racket of McDonald's surrounded them, making her head ache. She looked at the table, littered with paper napkins, plastic trays, and dripping ketchup containers, then noticed honey running down Seth's chin and automatically wiped his face. "I don't know why I couldn't go to dinner with Harris. He was going to do the buying."

"Yeah," Matt mumbled under his breath, but just loud enough for her to hear, "and *you* were gonna do the selling."

"You have to unbraid Sylvester," Grant reminded her.

Foster glared. "Don't you turn into a teenager on me now, Charlie. It's too late for that. Too many people have too much invested in you."

As she looked angrily away, he growled, "And I told you to eat, so eat!"

"Oh, yessir! Right away, sir!" Furious, she took a sip of milk from a carton, then picked up a tan lump of chicken and wolfed it down. "Private Railsberg, eating as ordered, sir!"

Foster swore under his breath, but left her alone, since she was doing as he said—even if under protest.

"I could have learned a lot from him," Charlie defended herself, swallowing a french fry. "He knows several people who might be interested in buying Sylvester."

"So he *said*." Matt's dark eyes flashed angrily. "If you just wanted to jump into the sack with the blankety-blank U.S. Olympic Team, you should've said so. We could've bought you a bus ticket. One way."

"Shut up!" she cried, "you just *shut up!*"

Seth broke the uncomfortable silence. "We didn't say grace," he ventured.

"You don't say grace in a place like this," Charlie told him.

"Oh, right," Matt said sarcastically, "we're too sophisticated now, is that it? Say grace, Seth."

"It's too late, we're half done," Grant objected.

"It's never too late," Foster said.

"Might do some of us some good." Matt gave Charlie a sideways glance as he bowed his head.

Still smoldering, but slightly ashamed of her behavior, Charlie followed suit. The noise of McDonald's seemed to recede a little. "Go on, Seth."

"God, we need a miracle," the little boy said earnestly. "Amen."

"Matt's leaning on me again," Charlie said to Sylvester as she carefully snipped the white thread securing one of his braids in place. Tugging the plait loose, she combed it out with a metal mane comb dipped in water with a little creme rinse. "Why does he do that, when he knows that makes me crazy?"

Sylvester snuffled eloquently, his eyes half-closed as he listened.

"You did great today," she told him. "I think even Mr. Foster was impressed. How would you like to live around here? Pretty ritzy, huh? But you'd deserve it."

She thought about driving home with an empty trailer, and her heart lurched a little. She knew Sylvester would have to be sold—the horse had great potential, she'd known it all along, and now other people were beginning to see it, too. Potential that could never be fulfilled standing around in John Foster's stockyards . . . but it was still going to hurt to say goodbye, it always did.

She hugged his neck as she stood on the packing crate. "I'll miss you, you big ox. And you'd better do good for whoever buys you—I want to see your name and picture in *Practical Horseman* someday. Maybe you can even make the Olympic team!"

Mention of the U.S. Equestrian Team made her think of Harris Pell again. She snipped another braid, remembering the look in Matt's eyes when he'd come up to her after the dressage test today. When she'd introduced him to Harris, he'd barely been civil. "He's jealous, Sylvester," she said, combing. "First he was jealous of *you*, now it's Harris Pell."

She remembered the scene at dinner. "Why does life have to be so complicated, Sylvester? Just as you begin to get something you wanted, something else happens to spoil it. Matt's being unreasonable, just like Daddy used to be . . ."

Snipping another plait, she remembered her father, how he used to come home angry and tired from working in the oilfields, or driving his rig, and not speak to anyone. He'd sit there in his chair, opening one beer after another, and finally, when he began to talk, it was always to complain . . . complain about how hard he worked, how nobody appreciated him, about how he was better than the other guys but somehow that was always overlooked.

When he finally ran down, he'd open yet another beer and look around the trailer, and something would be wrong—Seth's diaper was dirty, or they were having fried chicken *again*, or Lena was putting on weight. Then the yelling would start, and soon—

Charlie jerked herself out of painful memories, and combed out Sylvester's mane one last time. "There, now you look more like a horse than a Barbie doll."

Sylvester was asleep.

CHAPTER 19

Endurance Test

"Number 76 start, number 117 on deck, number 77 be ready," the Steward announced, reading from a clipboard. Charlie sat tensely on Sylvester, watching as a gray Thoroughbred, number 76, trotted out of the white-boarded starting area on Phase A, the Roads and Tracks. Ariane was next, on her chestnut mare. Foxfield was snorting and frothing, pawing frantically at the turf until Ariane jerked her reins and yelled at her.

"Get set, Charlie," Foster said tensely. Grant wiped her already-shining boots with a rag. Matt stood by, Seth sitting on his shoulders so the little boy could see.

"Good luck," Matt said.

"Thanks," she said, and called to Ariane, "Good luck!"

"Thanks!" Ariane said, as the frantic chestnut bolted out of the starting box.

"Now that's *just* what you don't want to do, Charlie! Start out at the trot, and watch your time! If you do this roadwork too fast, you won't have a horse left for the steeplechase or the cross-country! So watch your time. Thirteen minutes to the bridge should be about right . . . Charlie!'' Foster glared up at her. ''Are you paying attention?''

''Yessir,'' she said.

''Get ready, 77,'' the steward said, and Charlie moved Sylvester up.

''I hope you remember this course,'' Foster said. ''Did you study the map?''

''Yeah,'' Charlie said, holding Sylvester still. The big gelding had caught some of her nervousness and was quivering.

''They don't penalize you for being too early, but they do for being late. So keep an eye on that watch. Remember, white flag on your left, red on your right.''

''Okay,'' she said, abstractedly.

The Steward looked over at Foster. ''Once she starts, if you say or do anything—even wave—to tell her to speed up or slow down, she's eliminated.''

The old man subsided. ''Good luck, Charlie.''

''Go!'' said the Steward.

Charlie loosened the reins and Sylvester, relieved at the chance to move, catapulted out of the box as though it were a bucking chute. Foster threw his hands up in the air. ''The watch!'' he said to Matt. ''Did she get the watch?''

''She got it,'' Matt said. ''Relax, John, she's already slowing down.''

Charlie trotted along on Sylvester, enjoying the late morning air, the dappled shadows beneath the huge trees, the green turf underfoot. She could almost forget this was anything but a pleasant ride through the woods, along back-country roads—almost.

She glanced at her watch, saw she was almost to the bridge, and about thirty seconds behind time. Sitting down in the saddle, she nudged Sylvester into a slow canter.

Sylvester had never crossed a wooden bridge before, and snorted when he saw it. "No time to fool around, pal," Charlie told him, sitting down hard on the gray horse. The gelding minced on, trying to swerve when he heard the hollow clumping of his hooves on the planks.

Charlie slapped him behind the saddle with her jumping bat, and, skittering, he trotted on. "There, that wasn't so bad," she told him. "You're used to going through water now, not over it, right?"

Sylvester snorted, flicking forward his ears as they turned onto a sun-bathed dirt lane. Over on her right, Charlie could see a green field filled with sheep. "The East is pretty," she told the horse as they trotted along, "but so closed in. Sometimes I feel as though I'm surrounded by walls, here. I miss the mountains . . ."

Checking her watch, she urged Sylvester to a faster trot. "One more mile to go," she told him, feeling his neck to see if he was beginning to sweat. "Just one more mile, then the steeplechase."

"There, she's off!" Matt said, pointing. Sylvester, a flash of gray with a black-and-yellow smudge poised over his withers, was thundering along the turf of the steeple-chase course, heading for the first fence.

"Wow, she's moving!" Grant said, looking through Foster's old field glasses. "She's over the first fence!"

They watched the gray gelding as he flattened out across the course, galloping hard, flying over the brush jumps.

Foster checked his stopwatch. "She's really moving," he said, "it's gonna be close!" He bounced up and down on his heels, his leathery face creased with worry. "Too old for this at my age," he mumbled. "I wish I'd sent that consarned horse to the dog food factory."

"Over the third fence," Matt said. "I hope Sylvester doesn't hang a leg up. At this speed—"

"I hate kids," Foster continued his mumbled monologue, "I hate horses. Why I let myself get roped into this is beyond me . . . I can't take this kind of thing anymore, my left arm's starting to hurt, probably keel over with a heart attack . . ."

Matt took a beer out of his pocket, popped the top, then handed it to the old man. "Shut up, John."

Foster took a swig, though the worry lines around his eyes remained.

Sylvester came closer, heading for the finish, still going strongly. "I hope he can make it through the next Roads and Tracks," Matt said. "This is bound to take a lot out of him."

"It's taking a lot out of *me*," Foster said plaintively. "Why I ever—"

"She's over the last fence!" Grant yelled, turning and sprinting for the finish.

The others followed him, in time to see Sylvester, blowing hard, sweat springing out on his neck and flanks, trot away for Phase C, the second Roads and Tracks.

"How'd she do?" Matt asked Foster, who was examining his stopwatch.

"Three seconds below Optimum," he said. "No penalty points!"

"Good," Matt said. "That gives her some leeway, doesn't it?"

"No, the time for each Phase is independent of the others," Foster said. "She can't afford any time penalties in cross-country . . . not at this level of competition."

"We'd better get down to the vet check," Matt said. "If she stays on schedule, she'll be back in twenty minutes or so."

Carrying their equipment, they hastened across the green turf, ignoring the curious glances at their jeans, western hats, and boots.

"Here she comes!" Seth shouted. Charlie trotted over the top of the slope, through the electronic timers, and down to the vet check. Sylvester's nostrils were wide and red-rimmed as he breathed, and he was dark with sweat. White lather foamed between his hind legs. Charlie slid off him, panting herself.

"Let's move, we've only got ten minutes!" Matt said, leading him into the vet box.

"I've got the ice," Grant said, holding a sack of it against the horse's throbbing jugular. The two vets who had been standing back, watching Sylvester walk, moved in then. One checked Sylvester's respiration, the other listened to his heartbeat with a stethoscope.

After a minute the first vet straightened. "Okay here," he called.

The second vet, a slight young woman, pulled the earpieces of the stethoscope out of her ears, nodding. "He's cleared to go on."

Hastily they led the horse out of the vet box, then Foster sponged him with warm water, afterwards scraping moisture off his neck, back and chest with a metal blade. Seth, lower to the ground, sponged off his legs.

''You okay?'' Matt asked Charlie, not looking up from his examination of the bridle, girth, stirrup leathers, and breastplate for any weak points.

''Yeah,'' she said. ''I could learn to like this. How am I doing?'' She was rinsing her mouth out from a cup of water as she walked up and down so her legs wouldn't cramp.

''No penalty points in the steeplechase,'' Foster said tersely. ''Now you've just gotta make Optimum in the cross-country, honey.''

''Okay,'' she said.

''Six minutes,'' Matt warned. He finished wiping Sylvester's head with a damp towel, then picked up the horse's hooves, one by one, replacing the small traction studs screwed into his shoes with the larger ones designed for cross-country going. As he did each hoof, he examined the V-shaped frog for stones caught down in the narrow crevices. ''He's okay,'' he said.

By now Sylvester's breathing was returning to normal. Foster checked the two girths, then tossed Charlie back into the saddle, and she rode back for another brief once-over by the vets. Then she was next in line to enter the starting box.

The last minute of waiting seemed interminable. Charlie found that she was shaking—whether with tenseness or eagerness, she didn't know. ''Check your watch, honey,'' Foster said quietly.

She nodded, not shifting her gaze from the open field in

front of her, with its first jump, a comparatively low brush.

"Number 77," said the starter, checking his timer, "be ready. Five . . . four . . . three . . . two . . . one—GO!"

Sylvester shot out of the starting box like a racehorse, throwing up clods of turf.

Charlie started her watch as she headed the gelding for the brush, letting him settle into his stride, noting with satisfaction that his ears were pricked forward. He was eager to go. The brush flowed by beneath her smoothly, and she checked her course.

The Park Pavilion next. This obstacle was a jump into and out of a structure designed to look like an old-fashioned gazebo, with tall openings in its white latticework sides for the horse to go through the middle of the fake building. Some horses were thrown off by the sudden transition from light into darkness, but Sylvester leaped in, then out, with no hesitation.

Next the option fence. Sylvester thundered up to it, going too fast for the close-set, angled post-and-rails. Charlie sat back on him a little, working the bit in his mouth to get his attention and slow him down. After a moment of resistance, his strides shortened. She steered him for the first post-and-rail, saw his ears prick forward and knew that he'd noticed the combination.

Thrust of hindquarters and she was airborne. Charlie turned Sylvester's head slightly so he'd come down at the correct angle. Then the slight shock of landing, a single plunging stride, and she was up again. Shock of landing, and she leaned forward.

Now, she thought to the horse, through the position of

her body, her touch on the rubber reins, *now the wide corner fence!*

Sylvester went up and over like a bird. Charlie heard an excited whoop, and realized after a second that she'd made it herself. This was living! There was no more exciting feeling in the world than to be astride and controlling twelve hundred pounds of horseflesh on a rocketing, dizzying plunge over the green turf of Kentucky!

For a moment she allowed herself to savor the feeling, then she returned to business. She was here to *win,* not have fun . . .

Next was the black "table"—four feet high, over four feet wide and solid as a cement wall. Charlie gave the gelding plenty of leg. *Don't skim this one, Sylvester!*

Then they were over, galloping downhill. Ahead of her was the first bank, four feet high, leading down to a road, then another four-foot bank. Sylvester had the option of either landing on top and jumping off (called "banking" the obstacle) or leaping it entirely. Charlie sat down solidly in the saddle, giving him plenty of rein and leg.

Sylvester flew the first bank, touched down for three strides as he crossed the road, then leaped up the second bank. He "banked" this one slightly, pushing off it with his hindquarters.

As soon as she landed there was a ninety-degree left turn to another post-and-rail, then down the hill to the coffin combination. This was a much more difficult coffin than the ones she'd jumped before, as the horse had to leap a post-and-rail *downhill,* into the shadow of some trees, jump a ditch lying in that shadow, and jump out over another post-and-rail *uphill.*

Sylvester jumped the first fence well, but was taken

aback by the difficult-to-see ditch. He bobbled slightly, clearing it at the last moment, losing momentum. Charlie gathered up her reins, sending him on using legs, seat, and voice for encouragement. "Go!" she shouted, "*Go!*"

Sylvester went.

Fence number twelve, the bullfinch brush, was an easy fence, but the combination beyond it was the Lexington banks. She brought Sylvester around in a ninety-degree turn to the right, sending him leaping up, then two strides across on top of the wide bank. Then she was looking down at the terraced drop, yawning below like the plunge into the Grand Canyon. Charlie froze for a second, but even without her urging Sylvester was going, he was gathering himself, leaping out and down!

The shock of landing off the huge drop sent her sliding far forward, almost losing her seat and stirrups. She scrambled to regain her position as Sylvester plunged the two strides toward the bounce.

Then, just as she was in position again, he was taking off over the bounce. It was like riding a colossal rocking horse as the gray gelding swooped down, then immediately up again.

The water jump is next, Charlie thought, remembering the big drop down into the water. She tightened up for a second, remembering her moment of panic at the Lexington bank, then resolutely sent Sylvester on. If she betrayed fear now, the gelding would sense it. She remembered an old horseman's adage: *Throw your heart over, then jump after it*.

The water jump on the Lexington course made both of the other water jumps Charlie had taken look like puddle-hops. Coming up on it, the horse had to jump a seven-foot wide ditch, then, a stride later, a jump of two thick black logs with a height of about three-and-a-half feet. The log obstacle was high enough that a horse couldn't see that it was jumping down into water until the very last moment before take-off—a situation that invited a sudden refusal.

On the other side of the logs was a two-and-a-half foot stone dam down to the water level. Once in the water, the animal was required to take several strides, then leap up onto a table just above water level, off again back into the water, then jump a two-and-a-half foot bank out of the water.

After leaving the water, the horse had a bare two or three strides to a high, white angled post-and-rail with a drop on the other side.

The first time Charlie had seen the Lexington water jump, she'd remarked to Harris Pell that the people who designed Three-Day Event courses must all be sadists. At the time, they'd both laughed, but, as she galloped up the field toward the first ditch, it didn't seem a bit funny anymore.

Throw your heart over, Sylvester's drumming hooves seemed to say, *throw your heart over . . .*

Sylvester hurdled the ditch, landed, then raced on to the black logs. Charlie steadied him, urging him forward, and the gelding jumped—

—only to land with an enormous splash, stumble, then skid in the almost chest-deep water! Charlie was flung forward, then sideways, as Sylvester floundered, trying to stay up. Her hands went out, grasping for something, anything to keep her on the horse—

—and her right hand caught hold of his sopping mane. Charlie sank her fingers into the coarse hair, pulling herself back into the saddle. Sylvester hadn't stopped his forward motion, and neither of them, technically, had fallen. If she could get him going, she could still score a clean round.

"Come on!" she cried, using her legs and seat—*my stirrup, I've lost my left stirrup*—no matter, she was going, Sylvester was going, now, *now!*

With a huge leap, the gray vaulted up onto the tabletop. Ignoring her lost stirrup, Charlie drove him on again, off the tabletop, back into the water. A final heave up the bank, and they were out! Soaking and shaken, but out!

"Can't stop now, Sylvester!" she grunted, urging the horse forward, digging her left knee into the knee-roll of the saddle for security. The gray headed for the white post-and-rails, made a huge leap, and was over.

Once back on level ground, Charlie's left toe found the dangling stirrup without her having to look down. They raced on, and she realized that she'd lost her bat somewhere in the water. It didn't matter, though. She and Sylvester were a team, and she knew from the way his strides were coming that he was as eager to go, to win, as she was.

Almost there, she thought, checking her watch. *If I make up a few seconds I'll still be under Optimum Time with no faults.* Squeezing Sylvester with her legs, she asked for a little more speed, and got it.

"Good boy," she murmured. "You're the greatest."

The rest of the jumps: the black wall, the A,B,C post-and-rails combination, the park bench, the stone wall, all seemed to go by in a hazy, dreamlike effort. Charlie felt exhilarated to the point of euphoria. She was riding on instinct and nerve, riding like a wild thing, as she urged the horse to give her every bit of speed he could manage on the straightaways.

When Charlie and Sylvester swept through the electronic timers at the end, the crowd of spectators was cheering.

She pulled up the gray, and someone caught his bridle. Exhausted, she slipped off—and might have fallen, if someone hadn't caught her. It was Harris Pell, grinning from ear to ear as he kissed her on the cheek. "Congratulations! Wonderful round!" he said.

Even as he spoke, Charlie felt herself scooped into the air, then smelled tobacco. John Foster hugged her so hard her ribs almost cracked, speechless with delight. When he put her down, the boys swarmed onto her.

"Where's Matt?" she asked, standing up, looking around.

"He's got the horse," Foster said.

"Can I take you to the exhibitor's party tonight?" Harris Pell asked, touching her shoulder to get her attention.

This was the first she'd heard of any party, and Charlie stared at him blankly.

"No, you can't," Matt's voice interrupted. "She's busy."

Charlie glared at him, shocked by his open hostility. "Matt!" she said angrily, "don't start this stuff! You don't own me!"

She turned back to Harris Pell, who was smiling triumphantly at Matt. "I'm not invited to the party," she said to him. "But if I had been I'd be pleased to go with you."

"You're invited now, Charlie," he said.

"We have to walk Sylvester," she muttered, confused. "He'll colic if we let him stand hot."

"John's got him," Matt said brusquely, taking her arm and leading her after the horse. Seth and Grant were jumping up and down, patting Sylvester. Matt hurried Charlie over to them.

They were halfway back to the stable when a small entourage met them. Charlie saw with surprise that someone seemed to be sitting in the middle of the moving crowd, then realized the woman was in a motorized wheelchair. She was blonde and lovely, and only the tiny lines around her eyes and mouth betrayed her true age, somewhere in the late forties. The people surrounding her were riders, including Ariane.

"Ms. Railsberg!" she called. "Mr. Foster!"

"Yes, ma'am?" Foster tipped his hat respectfully. The woman in the expensively tasteful clothes had a quiet air of command that was immediately felt.

"Could you spare a moment, please?"

"Yes, ma'am." Foster nodded to her, then passed Sylvester's reins to Matt. "Keep him moving, son."

"I'm Mrs. Whitney Hyde," the woman said, holding out her hand to him, "Muffy Hyde. Delighted to meet you. And Ms. Railsberg."

Charlie ducked her head, then, self-conscious because of her sopping clothes, gingerly shook hands. "How do you do, ma'am."

"Ms. Railsberg," Muffy Hyde fixed her with an intent, measuring blue gaze, "that was a magnificent round. Where did you train?"

"Texas, ma'am."

"Yes, but with whom?"

"Mr. Foster, here."

Muffy turned to the old man, who explained, "I run a stockyards down in Marfa. Charlie's one of my wranglers.

She trained him herself. I was fixin' to sell him to the killers."

"And I understand Sylvester is for sale?"

"Yes, ma'am," both Foster and Charlie said together.

"Well, I'd love to talk with you about him. Could you both come to my house about five?"

"Yes ma'am. Where do you live?"

"The white house three miles north on this road. Any of the stewards can give you precise directions."

"Fine, ma'am," Foster said, tipping his hat again as she touched a control on the chair and it began to roll away.

The chair's motion halted after a second, though, and the woman turned back. "Oh, and by the way, there's an opening in the big barn now. I think Sylvester might be more comfortable there, if you'd care to move him."

"Thank you, Mrs. Hyde."

The chair glided smoothly away across the grass, followed by the entourage.

Charlie turned to a reporter who was standing nearby with a notepad. "Who is she?"

The man looked faintly surprised that she didn't know. "Mrs. Hyde? She's the main sponsor of this event. One of the wealthiest women in Kentucky."

CHAPTER 20

How the Other Half Lives . . .

Foster's old pickup rattled up the wide, horseshoe-shaped driveway. Beside him, Charlie sat looking at the sculptured grounds, the stone gateposts and walls, and the looming Southern mansion with her mouth open. "I should have put on my dress," she said to Foster. "They'll probably toss us out on our ears."

"Mrs. Hyde didn't strike me as that kind," Foster said. "There's rich people, and there's snobby rich people. I got the feeling that Muffy belongs in the first category."

"I hope you're right," Charlie said, as Foster stopped the truck in front of the white-columned portico. They got out, and Charlie looked back at the old vehicle. "What a contrast," she observed dryly.

As they approached the massive, wood-paneled door, it was opened by a butler. *A real, honest-to-God* butler! Charlie thought, giving the man a quick once-over. *I didn't think people still had them.*

"Mr. Foster? Ms. Railsberg? Please follow me."

They walked through a massive entry hall with a polished white marble floor and oak-paneled walls. Charlie stared around her, feeling as though she were on a movie set. *How can people go to the bathroom in a place like this?* she wondered. *It'd be like living in a museum or something.*

As they crossed the hall behind the butler, Ariane came out, greeting them with a warm smile. "Hi, there. Muffy's waiting for you. Come on in."

They followed the young woman into a good-sized room with carved, oak panels along the walls, a ceiling that must have been twenty feet high, and a massive marble-faced fireplace. Muffy Hyde was sitting poised on her couch, smiling. "Hello," she said, shaking hands with them again. "I'm so glad you could come. Please, sit down."

They stood poised uncertainly, until she waved them to seats. Charlie perched on the edge of the brocade chair, fervently thanking heaven that she'd had the foresight to wear her clean Levis. "I'm very impressed with Charlie's riding of Sylvester, Mr. Foster," Muffy said. "You must be very proud of her."

"She done it herself," Foster said.

"Well, I'm very interested in both your wrangler and your horse. If it's all right with you, I'd like to take Charlie on a little tour of my stables while we talk."

"Yes, but Sylvester belongs to Mr. Foster, Mrs. Hyde," Charlie said. "If you're thinking of buying him, you need to talk with him."

The blonde woman smiled gently as she slid over onto the seat of her motorized chair. "Yes, I know, but I always like to talk to the rider when I'm considering buying a horse. Ariane, maybe Mr. Foster would like some refreshment while we're gone?"

The young woman with the curly dark hair turned to Foster, who nodded. "Yes ma'am, a beer would be nice."

"Come on, Charlie, this way," Muffy directed, as she steered the chair out of the room.

Charlie, with one last nervous glance at Foster, followed her.

Mrs. Hyde didn't talk much during the tour, except to identify the areas as they reached them. Charlie saw the foaling barn and paddocks beyond, where mares grazed with their six-month-old colts and fillies by their sides. Then there was the stallion barn, each stall with its individual small, high-boarded paddock, where the glossy Thoroughbreds, Hanoverians and Swedish Warmbloods could be turned out.

There was a hot-walker, a motorized slow-turning octopus-like machine where one hooked a horse to one arm and the horse walked slowly, around and around, to be cooled out or stay in condition. And, inside a small shed, a horse shower, where horses could be sprayed with warm water—not the cold spurt from the hose, as they'd always bathed Sylvester.

They saw the jumping rings, and cross-country course. Two dressage arenas. Charlie had to keep reminding herself not to drool. The Horse Park had been one thing, but that was State-owned. The idea of such a facility as this being individually owned boggled her mind.

Finally they reached the large main barn, with its indoor arena centrally located. Charlie looked down the rows of oak-faced stalls, each with its brass nameplate, most with a glossy head poking over the doorway, and shook her head. "This place is *heaven*," she said. "Just heaven. Sylvester would fit in real good here, Mrs. Hyde. He's got nice stable manners, to go with everything else. He'd never give you a moment of trouble."

"Tell me about his training," she said, looking up at Charlie.

"Well, I did most of the early part. Then Mr. Foster started coaching me, 'cause he was in the cavalry. He's got a houseful of books and *Practical Horseman*. We read up on Eventing, and the guys I work with built me a course. Everyone helped."

"You read up," Muffy said evenly. "I see."

"Well, we were lucky that they had a lot of pictures of the jumps and all." She gave the older woman an earnest look. "I knew he was special the first time I saw him. There was something about Sylvester . . ."

"And you wanted to make him the best."

"Yeah!" Charlie said, surprised by the complete understanding she saw in the woman's eyes. "I mean, yes, ma'am. I *knew* he could do it. He had courage, and bottom."

"He certainly proved that today," Muffy nodded. "Both of you did. Tell me, Charlie, how do you think *you'd* fit in here?"

"What?" Charlie stared at her.

"I have an opening for a horse and a rider. I do this from time to time, as opportunity permits. Right now there are three young women living here, training with me and my instructors. Ariane is one of them, you've met her, and I believe you met my jumping instructor. I also have a dressage instructor. Both are ranked among the top teachers in the country." She waved a hand at a small house on the crest of a nearby ridge.

"My riders share that house while they live here. I pay a small salary, plus take care of living and training costs. Each rider is responsible for working and training two or three young horses, as well as the one they've brought. That gives them a wide range of horsemanship and training experience."

"But—" Charlie stammered, completely taken aback, "you don't know anything about me. What I'm like—"

"Oh, but I do," Muffy said, her blue eyes very serious. "I've seen you ride, and that tells me a lot. I can tell from the way you work with Sylvester, for instance, that you're just as interested in training horses as in riding them."

"Yes, I've always wanted to be a trainer," Charlie admitted, "but—"

"Do you realize you're in a position to possibly *win* this Event? After competing against riders who've been professionally coached in the sport for *years*?" She shook her head, a faint smile tugging at the corners of her mouth. "Charlie, do you have any idea at all what you've accomplished? What you *could* accomplish, given the training and experience I could give you here?"

Her hands were damp and cold from shock, and Charlie rubbed them distractedly against her jeans. "I don't—it was really Sylvester, he—"

"Oh, he's a talented animal, there's no denying that, but he could hardly have made it here on his own, could he? *His* accomplishment is *your* accomplishment."

Charlie hesitated for a long moment. *So this is what it feels like to be pulled in two,* she thought dismally. "Mrs. Hyde," she said finally, "I have two little brothers. You saw them. Our parents are dead, and I'm the one looking after them. Mr. Foster helps, but—" she shook her head distractedly. "They're real good around horses themselves, maybe I could—"

Muffy was already shaking her blonde head. "I'm not running a pony camp, Charlie. I'm talking about at least a year of serious, full-time training—with no distractions." She gazed off proudly across the vista of paddocks and jumps. "I've had Olympic riders and horses come out of this training facility. Riders who went on to become well-known trainers, some of them."

All the world right here on a silver platter, and I can't grab it, Charlie thought. She tried to change the subject. "Olympic horses—that's why Sylvester would be such a good horse for you, Mrs. Hyde. He's got the ability to go all the way, I think."

"Perhaps," Muffy said, her blue eyes intent. "With the right rider he might be able to. Charlie, you have a lot of raw talent—but that's not what people look for in selecting a trainer for their horses. They look for reputation. I'm offering you a chance to become a professional with a solid reputation. It could make a big difference in what you accomplish with your life. Will you please consider it?"

Charlie nodded, reluctantly. "Okay, I'll think about it. But tell me, why are you offering this? I could never pay you back."

Muffy looked down at her perfectly manicured hands for a moment, fiddling with a huge pearl and onyx ring. "How old are you, Charlie?"

"Seventeen," she said. "I'll be eighteen in a couple months."

The woman's mouth twisted. "I was two years older than you are now, when I fell. I was jumping, and my horse refused a stone wall. I landed on my spine. The doctors told me I'd never walk again. I've accomplished more than they ever expected, but they turned out to be right—I won't walk. And I can't ride."

She took a deep breath. "I was good, Charlie. I'd studied all my life, and it was a horrible blow. For awhile I managed to lose myself in helping my husband with his business, but when he died ten years ago, I felt . . . cast adrift. So I began giving young women the chance to make it, where I hadn't."

Muffy looked back up. "I don't expect to be paid back. It's a way of giving something more than just money to support a sport I love. Helping to coach the young riders I have here brings me back in contact with something I thought was gone from my life forever."

She reached out to grasp Charlie's cold fingers. "You're as good *right now* as I ever was. I want to see you reach your potential, Charlie!"

When they returned to the house, Mrs. Hyde graciously invited Charlie, Foster, Matt and the boys to attend the exhibitor's party that evening. The party was to be at the house, called Spindletop.

"I'm glad you made me buy a party dress to bring," Charlie told Foster as they climbed back into the truck. "Did you pack something to wear?"

"Yeah, I did. I remembered they usually have these kinds of shindigs connected with Events, so I brought my old uniform. Hope it still fits, after twenty-five years.

Guess Matt and the boys'll have to go rent tuxedoes for themselves."

As the truck turned out of the drive, Charlie said abruptly, "Mrs. Hyde offered me the chance of a lifetime, Mr. Foster."

"Yeah?"

"Yeah." Briefly she outlined her conversation with Muffy.

"Whew," the old man said when she'd finished, "I guess that's mighty tempting, isn't it?"

"Of course it is," she said sourly, leaning back in the seat and pulling her hat down over her eyes. "But I can't do it. The boys would wind up in Boys' Camp. Matt would have a hissy fit."

"He wouldn't be tickled pink, that's for sure."

"I *won't* leave the boys." Charlie clenched her fists. "Why did I even promise to think about it? I should have told her no, period, end of story. Then I wouldn't have to keep going over it like this!"

"Well, temptation makes fools of us all," Foster said, taking a philosophic bite out of a plug of tobacco.

They drove in silence for a moment, then Charlie's voice came out from under the Stetson, wistful. "Lordy, I could learn a lot there. People'd stand in line to have me train their horses. I could have my own place . . ."

"Charlie, remember what we came here for," Foster said warningly. "You think she'll buy the horse?"

"Maybe. But if *I* was part of the deal . . ."

"Well, you're not part of the deal, for two very good reasons. Seth and Grant." He hesitated for a moment, chewing thoughtfully. "But she's right, you know. You could be real good. You're better than I ever imagined you would be."

She tilted the hat back up to look at him, pleased and a little surprised to hear him say it. "Thanks."

They drove back to Spindletop, Muffy Hyde's mansion, a few minutes after seven. "Now remember," Foster cautioned, "we can't stay late. Charlie needs her rest, especially since she's got to braid Sylvester again tomorrow morning."

Charlie's eyes shone as she got out of the pickup, seeing the lights, hearing the music. "Wow," she murmured, taking Matt's arm, "swanky, huh?"

Matt, who was wearing a light blue tux with a black tie, nodded. "Do I look okay?"

"Super," she said, meaning it. At times she took Matt's good looks for granted, but when he was dressed up like this, she was struck by them all over again. "How do I look?"

"Pretty," he said, seriously. "I wish I had a picture of you the way you look tonight." He smiled. "I like the way you've got your hair brushed back. Shows off the earrings I gave you."

Foster and the boys rejoined them after parking the truck. The old man was very distinguished in his ancient black captain's dress uniform with its epaulets, tails, and gold braid on the sleeves and down the legs. Grant and Seth looked adorable in their little jackets, cummerbunds and bow ties.

"Well," said Foster, as they paused uncertainly on the doorstep, "are you tacky young'uns ready to go swank it up?"

"Ready as we'll ever be, I guess," Charlie said nervously. Suddenly her knee-length white dress trimmed with lace on the bodice and ruffles down the skirt seemed childishly unsophisticated and back-country. Through the enormous windows she could glimpse other women, all in long formal dresses and evening gowns. Charlie had never owned a long dress.

The butler opened the door, ushering them in, and the party walked into the enormous hall flanked by twin staircases and hesitated. "Some place," muttered Matt. "The Taj Mahal, right?"

Several people were looking at them and talking in low voices. "Here, Matt, want a chew?" Foster asked, proffering a brown package.

"Don't you dare!" gasped Charlie, horrified. "Mr. Foster, don't be gross! You can't chew tobacco here!"

Foster grinned brownly at her. "Who says?"

"Don't tell him what to do," Matt said.

"Are you two going to be impossible all evening?" Charlie looked at them, dismayed.

"I am if these people keep giving me those fisheyed stares," the old man said. "You ain't seen nothin' yet. I got my spurs on." He showed her.

"Oh, Lord!" Charlie stared frantically around the hall, wondering if she shouldn't just leave.

"Calm down, honey," Foster said, exchanging a glance with Matt. "Don't get in a tizzy, now. Why don't you go pay your respects to Mrs. Hyde, and thank her for inviting us."

Charlie nodded nervously, then started across the room. Matt watched her go, thinking that despite her inexpensive dress, she had more genuine class than any of the other young women he'd seen in Lexington. She moved gracefully through the crowd, shaking hands and nodding pleasantly when people recognized and congratulated her.

As Charlie made her way through the crowd toward the library, Matt saw Harris Pell take her arm and move in to talk with her, introducing her to the people. His manner was confident and intimate. Matt felt his blood pressure go up. "I guess to make it in this world, all you need is a team jacket and a cute ass," he told Foster, who was also watching.

"You mean a good seat," Seth corrected.

"Uh, right." Matt nodded at the little boy, then looked back at Foster. "I just can't take too much more of this—she's going faster and farther away every minute."

"She's a hard dog to keep under the porch," the old man agreed solemnly. An elegant older lady near him turned and stared at Foster, her eyes widening. Matt smothered a grin in spite of himself.

Muffy Hyde was resplendent in a white silk evening blouse and black velvet skirt. Around her neck she wore a heavy necklace of gold and onyx, with matching earrings. "Charlie!" she called, as she spotted the young woman, beckoning her into the library, where she was holding court.

The crowd parted respectfully at her gesture to allow the newcomers through. Charlie and Harris Pell came over to stand in front of Muffy. "Here you are!" she said. "I sent Harris to find you. I want you to meet some friends of mine that saw you ride today. Mrs. Van Husen, Mr. and Mrs. Bates McKee, Mrs. Lenore Campbell, and Mrs. Stone. This is Charlene Railsberg."

Charlie dutifully shook hands with each of them, wondering if she'd remember even one of all those names.

Mrs. McKee smiled at her. "If you win tomorrow, Charlene, then what?"

"Whatever happens tomorrow, I'm offering her a place in my barn," Mrs. Hyde told them.

"My daughter would kill for the chance to train here," Mrs. Stone said, with more than a trace of envy.

Ariane smiled at her. "Why do you want to sell Sylvester? He's such a nice horse. I saw your little brothers walking him. I'd never dare let my little sister near Foxfield."

"If we sell him for a good price," Charlie told her, "I can prove to the folks back home that I have what it takes to be a real trainer."

"Did you think over what we talked about?" Muffy asked.

"It's an awful lot to think about . . ." Charlie hedged. *Say no, tell her no, say no right now!* she told herself, but somehow, her mouth wouldn't obey her brain.

"What did Mr. Foster say?" Muffy asked.

"He said I was better than he thought," she answered.

Just then another guest came up to pay his respects, and Mrs. Hyde turned away. Charlie turned at a touch on her arm to find Harris Pell still beside her. "You look terrific," he whispered.

"Thanks." She smiled at him.

"I'm gonna be down here this fall, too. Betamax needs a few more schooling clinics before he moves up. Why don't you train with me? I could have you at Advanced level in no time."

"I have a better idea," Charlie told him. "Why don't *you* buy my horse?"

"You think we'd make a good team?"

Charlie grinned. "Think of the stir you'd make when they announce Sylvester and Tweedy now entering the ring."

Harris laughed. "You crack me up, Charlie. You're not like anyone I ever met."

"Ditto," she told him. The young man leaned over and gave her a quick kiss before she could move away.

"Think about it," he said. "We could have a lot of fun together."

Over his shoulder, she saw Matt, Foster and the boys making their way through the crowd into the library. Matt was glowering. *He must've seen Harris kiss me,* Charlie thought sourly. *If he says anything in front of everyone . . .*

"Hello, Mr. Foster, welcome to Spindletop again," Muffy said, holding out her hand to the old man. He shook it gravely, then introduced Matt and the boys.

In the brief silence that followed, Mrs. Hyde said to Foster, "I'm so impressed with the job you and Charlie have done with Sylvester, Mr. Foster. You must love horses very much to work with them so well."

The old man's eyes twinkled mischievously. *Oh, no!* Charlie thought. *He's gonna be impossible again!* "Not me, ma'am," Foster was replying to Muffy. "A horse has less personality than a crow, he's more delicate than a hummingbird, less efficient than a bicycle, and more expensive than a floozy. What I *love* is a mule."

To Charlie's surprise, Muffy wasn't offended. She threw back her head and laughed. "Aptly put, Mr. Foster! I have several mules on the place, and I must say that they're far easier keepers than the equine tenants."

Matt edged over beside Charlie, still looking daggers at

Harris, who smiled smugly. ''I'm leaving,'' he whispered to her, turning around to do just that.

Charlie caught his arm. ''Matt, wait.''

''Well, boys,'' Muffy was saying to Grant and Seth, smiling, ''what do *you* think, should your sister stay here and train horses for me?''

The boys looked at her, stunned. ''Charlie?'' Grant said.

''Our sister?'' Seth looked over at her, frightened.

''I didn't tell them yet, Mrs. Hyde,'' Charlie said swiftly.

''What's this all about?'' Matt asked, moving quickly over to put a hand on Grant's and Seth's shoulders. As he did so, a man in a red velvet dinner jacket jostled him, and without thinking, Matt shoved back.

Harris Pell smiled patronizingly at him as he took Charlie's arm to steer her away. ''We'll see you later, and, hey, try to be civilized, okay? You're not out on the prairie now. Look around, you'll get the idea how to act. You wouldn't want to embarrass Charlie when—''

Even as Charlie stepped away, trying to disengage her arm, Matt reared back and slugged Harris Pell, who went down on his rear with a thump. Scrambling up, he punched Matt hard in the stomach, and Matt responded with another punch to Pell's jaw. At the last second Harris ducked, throwing a right for Matt's ear.

''Get him, Matt! Deck that sucker!'' Grant yelled, as Matt gave the Easterner two quick punches to the stomach. Harris was no pushover, though, and almost immediately waded back in, his expression ugly.

Charlie stood frozen in horror as the two young men grappled with each other, then went down in a thrashing, slugging welter on the library carpet. *This can't be happening!* she thought, stunned. *What am I gonna do?*

Before she could think of anything, John Foster strode over to the buffet table, grabbed the gargantuan sterling punch bowl, and, turning, tossed its contents over both combatants. The splash of icy champagne punch made both fighters gasp as they rolled apart.

''Works for dogs, too,'' Foster said to Muffy, as he grasped Matt and hoisted him to his feet, while Mr. Bates McKee restrained Harris.

Charlie took the boys by the hand. ''Come on, Grant, Seth,'' she said, setting her jaw and holding her head high, ''let's go home.''

With hands that still shook, Charlie unlocked the door to the motel room. Her brothers staggered in and collapsed on their bed. Seth's eyes closed immediately. ''That,'' she said in an icy tone as Matt followed them in, ''was a *wonderful* evening. Thanks a bunch!''

''Nobody wanted to go there but you,'' Matt said, yanking his still-damp bow tie off and unbuttoning his ruffled shirt.

''Why did you even come here with me, Matt?''

He sat down on the other bed. They could hear Foster brushing his teeth in the adjoining room. Matt ran a hand through his hair, then looked up wearily. ''I figured you'd come here to Kentucky and whip the world, and that would get it out of your system. Instead,'' his eyes flashed with anger, ''you're getting *hooked* on this rich, horsey crapola.''

''Hooked on what?'' she demanded. ''Wanting to be good at something? Everyone knows that you walked out on that football scholarship—what were you afraid of? Wanting to be good?''

He glared at her, and she knew she'd struck a nerve. ''I didn't want to be owned,'' he said.

''But you don't mind doing the owning, do you? As long as it's me you're trying to hogtie and brand.''

He lunged up off the bed and grabbed her shoulders. For a moment his fingers dug into her, hard, and she was afraid, then he dropped his hands abruptly. ''This has really been a fun trip, Charlie, watching you sell out.'' He turned and headed for the adjoining door into his and Foster's room. ''I'm going home.''

The door slammed behind him.

CHAPTER 21

Taking Chances

Charlie stood listening as Matt told John Foster goodbye, then there came the sound of the motel room door closing. She heard the faint scuffle of his footsteps on the parking lot outside, then they, too, faded into silence.

Biting her lip, she turned and began undressing Seth, who was so tired he barely woke up enough to use the bathroom when she steered him in there. She carried him out in her arms, laid him on the bed, and pulled the covers over him, bending down to kiss his cheek.

Then, quite suddenly, Charlie found she was crying.

Covering her face with her hands, she tried to stop the tears, but she felt as though there were an entire ocean of them inside her, wanting to pour out.

"Don't cry," Grant said groggily, sitting up.

Charlie swiped at her face with the backs of her hands. "You know me, I never cry. If you're awake, get in your pajamas and brush your teeth."

Grant began undressing, slowly, while she changed into jeans and a shirt. "We're staying together, aren't we?" he asked.

"Of course we are," she said. "You know I'd never let you and Seth go to Boys' Camp. I've always taken care of you, and I always will, until you're grown up."

"Why are you getting dressed? Where are you going?"

"I'm taking Foster's truck back to check on Sylvester one more time," she said. "I want to make sure his legs haven't filled up."

"It's late," he said.

"Not really, it's only ten. If just seems late, 'cause so much happened today."

"I'll say." On his way to the sink, toothbrush in hand, he turned back. "Charlie?"

"Yeah?"

"You didn't really want to stay here, did you?"

She couldn't meet his eyes as she picked up Foster's keyring. "Of course not."

After calling out to Foster where she was going, she kissed the boys goodnight and left. She drove slowly to the Horse Park, cautious on the unfamiliar roads. Parking outside the big barn, she went in.

Sylvester was lying down in his stall, all four legs stretched out, fast asleep. "Hi," Charlie said, "did you have a rough day too?"

The gelding's eyes opened and he raised his head to look at her, then scrambled up with a lurch and a heave. Charlie went into the stall to check his legs, found them satisfyingly cool and bony to the touch; no inflammation or heat. She checked his back, then his girth area. Sylvester turned around to bump her with his nose, a rare caress, and she hugged him, hard, grateful for any sympathy. The tears came welling up again, and she began to sob in earnest.

Matt, she thought, *Matt—I've lost my chance, and now I've lost you, too . . .*

Minutes went by while she leaned there, until Sylvester made a rumbling noise in his throat, then moved toward the door of his stall. Charlie turned to find Matt standing there, watching her, wearing his old clothes, his shirt unbuttoned and streaked with sweat. His duffel bag was tossed nearby.

She stared at him as though he were an apparition, wondering if she'd lost her mind.

"Matt?" she said, shakily.

He looked closely at her as she wiped her hands over her face. "You crying? I didn't think you knew how."

"I'm learning tonight," she said, expecting a quick retort, but Matt was silent, his eyes never leaving hers. "I thought you were leaving."

"I did," he said. "Caught a ride with a guy heading for Oklahoma City. Nice guy. I'd have been home tomorrow night. I got nearly ten miles out of town, before I told him to pull over. He thought I'd lost my mind, and can't say as I blame him."

He scuffed the toe of his old Tony Lamas into the packed clay of the aisle. "Caught one ride on the way back, but I had to run the last two miles or so. I was gonna sack out in the tack stall."

"Why?" She came over to the doorway, leaning her arms on top as she watched him. "Why did you come back?"

He shrugged. "Couldn't leave. Had to know how you

did tomorrow. I came this far, so . . ." he dug the toe of his boot into the hard dirt again.

"Well, thank you," she said. "I'm glad you came back."

"I was thinkin' what you said . . . about me not minding doing the owning . . . and, Charlie, I *was* out of line. But when I saw you with that Olympic guy . . ." he shrugged again. "It made me kinda crazy, I guess. I'm sorry about tonight."

Charlie gazed at him for a long moment. "Matt, do you honestly think I'm so dumb I couldn't see right through Harris Pell and his little line? Do you think I could ever *care* about somebody like that?"

"I dunno." He laughed a little, but it was not a sound of amusement. "John and me, we see you flyin' off, never looking back, and we're already missin' you. I really wanted you to succeed, I really did, but when it actually started . . . I dunno . . ."

"You wanted me to, but you didn't think I could?"

"Yes I did, I knew you could do it. But seein' it happen scared me, Charlie. I'm scared of change. Always have been. That's part of the reason I didn't go on with the football. It would've meant change, and—" he shrugged again. "I like my life, you see. I like Marfa, Texas. It's a nice town. I kind of belong there . . . like it's a niche somebody carved out just for me."

"Well, I like Marfa, too," she said. "Kentucky certainly isn't my niche. I learned tonight that I don't belong here, I never could be like Harris and those people who never have to think about money 'cause it's always there."

"But you could learn a lot here, working for Mrs. Hyde." His dark eyes were intent. "Couldn't you?"

"Yes," she admitted. "But it's not in my cards, or something."

He swung open the stall door, walking in until he stood facing her. "*You're* in *my* cards, that's all I'm sure of. I don't want to lose you, Charlie. You're the only girl I ever wanted to marry."

She looked up at him for a long minute. "Did I say I wouldn't marry you?" Her heart was beating so hard she thought that probably he could hear it. She could see a little pulse throbbing up under his jaw, felt a sudden urge to touch it.

Her words took a moment to penetrate. "You *will?*" He sounded surprised.

"Well, not right this minute, after all, I'm still too young. But my word's good. Want me to write you an I.O.U.?"

"Charlie . . ." Matt pulled her against him, holding her tightly, stroking her hair. Charlie could smell his sweat, feel the bare skin of his chest beneath her cheek. His heart was racing like hoofbeats. Slowly her arms went around him, returning the embrace.

"I could be as good as they are, I could be," she said, her face muffled against him.

"You're perfect," he said, his breath tickling her ear. "Perfect. I love you."

The warm dampness of his skin, the muscled strength of his body made Charlie feel lightheaded, almost dizzy, the way she'd felt during the last of the cross-country. She tipped her head back to look up at him, knowing he would kiss her if she did, wanting him to.

Matt's mouth was soft on hers at first, then gradually, as she responded, he became more urgent, demanding, parting her lips insistently. He stroked her hair, her neck, ran his fingers along her shoulder, and everywhere he touched she could feel her skin come alive beneath his. Her awareness of him was so complete, exciting, creating in her a warmth that made her legs go weak.

When he raised his head finally she was sorry, she had wanted it to go on and on—but something made her move back and away, even though losing the touch, the warmth of his body against hers, was something close to physical pain.

Matt took a step after her, but stopped when she held up her hand. "No, Matt. I don't think we'd better."

He took a deep breath, jammed his hands in his pockets, turning away. "Okay, Charlie," his voice was rough, unsteady, "I wouldn't want you to do anything you don't want to. Anything you'd be sorry for later."

She wanted to go back to him then, touch him, hold him, but forced herself to open the stall door, walk a few steps away. Her heart was beating so fast and hard that it hurt. "It's not that I don't *want* to, Matt. I don't think I ever knew before tonight that I could want something this much. But . . . I take my risks on the cross-country course, not with other people's lives."

He leaned over the stall door, gazing at her intently, but she could see from his expression that he didn't catch her meaning. She laughed a little angrily as she sank down onto a bale of hay. "If my mom hadn't taken a risk one night with Charles Railsberg, *I* wouldn't be here. Or maybe I'd be John Foster's daughter, and Mom would still be alive. Who knows? But I'm not about to make that kind of mistake at seventeen, the way she did."

She bit her lip. "I never knew anyone could make me

feel like that, and for a moment there, I was real tempted." She took a deep breath. "This must be my day for temptations."

"Charlie . . ." he opened the door, bolting it after him, then came over to sit down beside her on the bale of hay. "Hey, it's all right." Very gently he put his arm around her, sitting without moving until she finally relaxed.

"I never felt like that before," she repeated softly. "Have you?"

"Not like that."

"I must admit," she began to smile, "that kissing you was even better than going cross-country today. I never thought I'd be able to say that about anything."

Matt looked at her. "You just wait," he promised. "You ain't seen nothing, yet."

"I will wait," she said, "breathlessly. But right now, let's go back to the motel." The double meaning of the phrase under these circumstances struck Charlie suddenly, and she began to giggle shakily. She felt lightheaded, almost drunk.

"Come on, honey. You're tired." Matt helped her up, his arm strong around her shoulders, and, together, they walked out to the pickup. "Let me drive," he said. "You need all the rest you can get, if you're gonna win tomorrow."

"If only I could," she whispered. "Oh, Matt, if only I could!"

Charlie tightened Sylvester's girth as she sat on him, holding him steady with her right hand, as she tugged the billet straps up one more notch. "This is it, Sylvester," she told the gelding, "we don't want the saddle coming loose while you're in midair."

The gray gelding snorted, then pricked up his ears to look around at the melee in the practice area. Horses soared over jumps, one behind the other, sometimes barely missing other competitors as they landed. Charlie was amazed that there seemed to be few actual collisions.

"Let's warm up," she told the gray, nudging him into a trot, then a canter. After a few minutes she took him over the two practice jumps, one a spread, the other a high jump. He went willingly, but Charlie could tell he was still tired from the previous day's effort. Quite frankly, she was, too. That was why the stadium jumping on the third day was often the downfall of many competitors—Endurance Day took so much out of them and their horses that they got careless, made mistakes—or simply had nothing left to give.

After warming up, she saw there were only three competitors to go before her turn, so she trotted in circles near the entry gate, then pulled Sylvester up to rest for a moment.

"Charlie," a voice called, and, turning, she saw Muffy Hyde's chair part the crowd of bystanders near the In-Gate.

"Hello, Mrs. Hyde," she said. "I'm sorry about last night."

Muffy smiled and made a dismissing gesture. "Forget it, it wasn't your fault. Actually, it turned out to be one of the more interesting parties I've ever given. And, from what I hear, Harris was way out of line in what he said to your young man."

"He was," Charlie admitted. "But Matt is too quick on the uptake, sometimes."

"Aren't we all, sometimes?" She looked up at Charlie, her blue eyes very direct. "Have you thought it over?"

"Yes," she said miserably, "it's really the chance of a lifetime, but I don't belong here, Mrs. Hyde."

Muffy's blue eyes grew stern. "That, young lady, is entirely beside the point. Nobody is suggesting you spend the rest of your days in Kentucky horse society. The question is, do you belong *there*." She gestured at the arena. "Don't throw away your gift, Charlie!"

The younger woman shook her head, feeling tears threaten again. "I can't, people need me too much. But I still have to find a buyer for Sylvester."

"Charlie, if he finishes sound, I can name you ten people who will buy him without a second's delay. But simply selling him won't make you a trainer—not the kind of trainer you could be."

"Number 77, Sylvester Stallone, on deck," the announcer said.

Charlie picked up her reins. "I have to go," she said. "Thank you for everything, Mrs. Hyde."

As she reached the In-Gate, Harris Pell came riding out. "Hi, Charlie," he said. "I only had one rail down, so I'm the one to beat. You'll have to go clean, or I take it."

Charlie shrugged. "After cross-country? This'll be a snap, Tweedy."

The young man rolled his eyes. "Are you staying in Kentucky? Going to let me keep you company?"

"No, and no," Charlie said. "You've got too many other girls on the string, Tweedy, to worry about a little hick from Marfa, Texas."

He looked disappointed, but shrugged and rode on. Charlie knew he might stay disappointed for all of five minutes—which was about how long it would take him to find consolation with someone else.

"Our next entry, number 77, Sylvester Stallone, a gray gelding from Marfa, Texas, owned by John Foster, and ridden by Charlene Railsberg," the announcer said.

Taking a deep breath, Charlie trotted Sylvester into the jumping arena.

"There she is!" Grant cried, pointing. John Foster, Seth and Matt craned their necks as they stood at the rail of the huge ring, watching Charlie make her circle before beginning her round.

"Well," said a woman's voice, "you must be very special people."

Matt and Foster turned to see Muffy Hyde sitting beside them in her chair. "What makes you say that, ma'am?" Foster asked.

"Charlie's a good rider, but she's given up her chance to be a great one."

Matt glanced back at Charlie uneasily, remembering her muffled words last night: "I could be as good as they are . . . I could be."

The whistle sounded, and Charlie turned the gelding to go through the electronic timers, heading for the first jump, a double oxer with brush between the rails. Sylvester's ears flicked forward and back as Charlie collected him, then he soared over the fence.

Charlie sent him on toward the next jump, two stone gateposts with white rails between. Sylvester flew it like a bird, bringing a sigh of delight from the crowd, then a spontaneous ripple of applause.

"She knows *what* to do instinctively," Muffy Hyde

said, "but to really succeed, she's got to learn the reasons *why*. That's what she could learn here, with me. If you take this away from her, she'll never be the same."

"I guess we know Charlie better than you do," Matt said defensively, but her words touched an uncomfortable chord of truth within him.

"You know Charlie," she said, "but I *was* Charlie."

Sylvester thundered up to the third jump, a huge green-and-red painted oxer. The fence had a double set of rails spaced a few feet apart, thus providing a slight spread for the horse, as well as height. Charlie urged him toward it, leaning forward to give him maximum rein for the take-off.

"She's over it!" Grant said excitedly. Seth let his breath out in a whoosh.

Matt watched as Charlie went on to take the diagonal spread, the picket gate, made a difficult 180° turn to approach the one-stride in-and-out, then sent Sylvester hurtling over the two high, natural wood post-and-rails. Next came a brush and white rails jump flanked on either side by two red-brick wishing wells. Sylvester didn't like the look of them, slowing as he approached the fence, but Charlie never wavered, sending the gelding on so positively that he jumped beautifully.

"She's good," Matt found himself mumbling. "She's *really* good."

He hadn't realized anyone could hear him until Foster said, "She sure is."

"But, John," Matt shook his head, feeling a need to protest—even though the old man had said nothing further, "I can't lose her now, I *can't*."

"Sometimes," Foster said quietly, "you've gotta let go

to hang on to something. I watched her momma lose her dreams, one by one. It haunts me to this day, Matt."

In the ring, Charlie turned Sylvester sharply to get in straight at the next fence, a high obstacle with solid-looking planks instead of rails. Several competitors had knocked it down during the competition, but the gray gelding never put a foot wrong, clearing it with inches to spare. They could see Charlie's face clearly as she came over it, white with strain and exhaustion.

The next jump was a wide spread, and Sylvester made it look easy. "Just a couple more, honey," Matt heard Foster mumble. "Hold it together!"

A medium oxer gave Sylvester no trouble, and Charlie turned him toward the final combination, a close-set triple. Sylvester rounded the corner, heading for it, then suddenly slipped, stumbled, then picked himself back up.

Charlie was thrown forward, as the crowd gasped. She recovered, but her timing was off—she sent the gray toward the triple in a rush.

"Too fast!" Foster whispered, clenching his fists. "He'll get in too close!"

Sylvester went up in a huge leap, the angle of his body nearly vertical as he thrust himself over the obstacle. Charlie got "left," barely managing to give the horse enough rein to extend his neck to land.

The crowd groaned. Collision with the next fence seemed inevitable.

But Sylvester recovered himself as Charlie gave him more rein, taking off correctly for the final two fences, jumping them clean!

"She did it!" Seth and Grant screamed, jumping up and down, "she did it!" This time they weren't alone in their applause; everyone in the crowd was cheering wildly. Matt found himself pounding John Foster's back, his voice choked as he yelled something inarticulate. Tears sparkled in the old man's eyes.

"She did it! *He* did it!" Foster sputtered. "And to think I was gonna shoot that ugly sonofagun! I ain't never kissed a horse in my life, but I feel like kissin' that one!"

Muffy Hyde shook her head. "That horse saved her from an ugly crash just then. She could have been badly hurt, even killed." She smiled and nodded. "I'm going to have to buy Sylvester. He deserves the best, after that."

"Ladies and gentlemen, a clean round for number 77, Charlene Railsberg on Sylvester Stallone. With her clean round over the cross-country yesterday, that gives her an overall score of 51.9, to make her our new Preliminary Champion!"

Amid the renewed applause, Foster smiled at Muffy Hyde. "I believe that we can come to some reasonable settlement in response to your offer, ma'am. Just let me confer with my major stockholders, here." Throwing an arm around Matt's shoulders, he drew him and the boys away from the grandstand area, and all four bent their heads together.

Matt, Seth and Grant ran up to Charlie, who had already dismounted and was loosening her girth. Despite her victory, she looked upset. "You won! You won!" the boys yelled.

"*He* won." She patted Sylvester's neck gratefully, her expression still troubled. "I messed up. I didn't see that patch of mud."

"Hey!" Matt said, turning her to face him, "That's enough of that! You *both* won. You helped each other out, and that's the way it should be!" He hugged her, hard, then picked her up and swung her around until she began to laugh, breathlessly, throwing her arms around his neck.

"All right! All right! I won!" she gasped. "Where's Foster?"

"I'm here!" the old man said, from behind her. She turned to find him waving a long blue piece of paper at her. "*And,* we got what we came for, and then some!"

"Let me see that!" She took the check and stared at it, her eyes wide. "Ohmigosh! Thirty thousand dollars!"

"Yup," said Foster proudly.

"Is that a lot?" Seth wanted to know.

Charlie began to laugh hysterically, hugging him until the little boy squeaked in protest. "Yes, Seth, that's a *lot* of money!"

She grabbed Grant and pulled him into the embrace. "They'll never split us up, now!"

Sylvester put his nose down to look at her, as if asking what was happening. "You've got a new owner, buddy," she said, stroking his neck, "someone who will help you go all the way to the top. Muffy knows what she's doing, Sylvester."

"He'd do better with you riding him," Foster said.

Charlie looked up at him, thinking he was being sarcastic, but realized he was serious. She frowned, confused.

"I mean it, honey," Foster said. "You'd better stay here and help him out, or he might end up dog food after all."

Matt was nodding at the old man's words, and so were Seth and Grant. She stared at the four of them incredulously. "What?"

"We prayed for a miracle this week, we got it, and I

don't see any call to turn our backs on it. That'd be like telling God 'thanks, but no thanks.' " Foster smiled. "Right?"

"I don't fit in with these people," she said, softly.

"That don't matter. A year from now, *they'll* be tryin' to fit in with *you.*" The old man sighed. "I seen a lot of waste, Charlie, a lot of waste. I don't want to see that happen to you."

"Matt?" She turned to look at the younger man, stunned. "Matt . . ."

"Matt's a good man, and time ain't gonna change that. You two weren't gonna tie things up right away anyhow."

Matt nodded confirmation. "He's right, Charlie. I'm willing to wait, you know that. And if this is the best place for you to be for awhile, then I'm sayin' go for it."

"Grant? Seth?" She looked at her little brothers, her eyes beginning to sting.

Grant nodded. "We talked about it, and we decided that we could look after Mr. Foster just fine, Charlie. We won't let him mess the place up. He says he's even gonna build us a regular bedroom in the house!"

"We'll make him say grace every night," Seth added.

"But—" she hesitated, clearly torn.

"I did a pretty good job bringin' you up, Charlie. Think what I can do with the boys," Foster said. "This is my chance, too, Charlie. Let me take it, honey. I won't let you down—or them, either."

Charlie turned to Matt. "Should I do it, Matt?"

"This is the best thing ever happened to you, Charlie," he said. "A chance you'll never get if you stay in Marfa. I tried to hold you back, but that was wrong. You've made

Sylvester a champion, and that makes you one, too. I'll be rooting for you."

She hugged him, hard. "I love you, Matt. That won't change, ever."

"And now for the presentation of awards in this Preliminary Three-Day Event here at the Kentucky Horse Park," the announcer's voice said. "In first place, our new Preliminary Champion, we have Charlene Railsberg, riding number 77, Sylvester Stallone. Sylvester is owned by John Foster, of Marfa, Texas."

Charlie laughed, as she threw her arms around John Foster, near tears. "No he's not, not anymore! And to think you guys will have to rattle that empty trailer clear back to Marfa!"

Foster spat tobacco juice. "Oh, it won't be empty. I got Mrs. Hyde to throw in a mule."

"Number 77 to the ring, please," the announcer said.

"Lordy!" Charlie turned back to hastily tighten Sylvester's girth. "I've got to get out there!"

Matt boosted her into the saddle, and she cantered back into the arena, to take her place at the head of the line-up, giving Harris Pell a dazzling smile as she passed him.

The stewards had rolled a red carpet out onto the grass, and an attractive dark-haired woman in a silk dress came out, escorted by the President of the Ground Jury, the ranking judge at the Event. Charlie dismounted and a steward held Sylvester, while the woman, introduced as the wife of the Lieutenant Governor of Kentucky, shook her hand and congratulated her on her victory. Then she handed Charlie a large silver trophy, while the steward pinned a big blue rosette to Sylvester's headstall.

"Thank you, thank you all," Charlie said, shaking

hands with the judge and the steward. The steward gave her a leg back up onto Sylvester, then handed her the trophy.

"If you will lead the winning riders in a victory gallop, Ms. Railsberg," the man said.

Charlie neck-reined Sylvester one-handed, since she held the trophy in her right hand, and the gelding responded with all his old stock horse quickness, wheeling around on his haunches, then launching into a gallop around the perimeter of the ring. The other riders had to spur their horses to keep up with her.

"*Yeeehah!*" she whooped, as she saw Foster, Matt and the boys standing on the rail yelling, waving, and clapping. "*We did it!*"

Charlie stood in the stableyard at Spindletop, saying goodbye, as John Foster loaded his new mule into the old Stidham. Dawn was softening the sky, its faint light turning the hilltops blue over the mist.

"I'll write to you every day," she told Grant and Seth. "Now you have to write me at least once a week, promise? Grant, you'll help Seth, won't you?"

"Sure I will," he said. "Don't worry about us, Charlie. We get along with Mr. Foster real good, and Matt says he'll be coming by every day."

"Well, okay," she said, trying not to cry, as she hugged them one more time, then watched as they ran off to hop into the old pickup.

"I'll be seein' you, Charlie!" Foster said, coming over to hug her. He cleared his throat. "You take care, now."

Finally only Matt was left. Charlie was unable to hold back tears as he held her, kissing her so thoroughly that

Grant and Seth whistled and hooted out the window of the pickup. "Shut up over there, you guys!" Matt called, then kissed her again. "I'm gonna miss you, Charlie. I'll write, I promise."

She nodded, unable to speak.

"Love me?" He held her shoulders and looked down at her.

She nodded again. "Always," she whispered.

"Be seein' you at Christmas, Charlie." He turned, walking away quickly.

She whirled and ran back into the oak barn, not wanting to stand and watch while they drove away. When she reached the stall with the new brass nameplate that read "Sylvester Stallone," she stopped, unable to go on. After a moment, something nudged her damply over the top of the door—Sylvester, water dribbling off his lower lip from his recent drink.

Charlie buried her face in the horse's silky neck, holding him tightly. His warmth comforted her, and after awhile, she was able to let go.

Matt walked up to the stock trailer, silently helped John Foster fasten the security chains. The new mule snorted and stamped. "Come on, John," he said impatiently, seeing that the old man was looking up the hill to the expensive barn, its outlines rosy in the first light. "Let's go while the going's good." His voice was strained.

Foster nodded philosophically. "You can't clip an eagle's wings and put it in a hen house, Matt."

"Oh, shut up, John." Jerking open the door of the pickup, Matt climbed in. Seth settled onto his lap.

Foster walked around to the driver's side, saw the two

small faces looking at him expectantly. ''Lord, I hope I haven't made a mistake.''

He climbed behind the wheel, as Grant said, ''Of course you haven't. We'll take just as good care of you as Charlie did—she even gave me her recipes for stew.''

The old man groaned aloud, hearing Matt's chuckle. ''Charlie says we're her Marfa farm team now,'' the older boy continued.

''I got the check right here to prove it,'' Foster said, patting his pocket with one hand, while he fumbled for his keys with the other.

''You think we can find another Sylvester by the time Charlie gets home for Christmas, Mr. Foster?'' Grant asked.

''Or maybe Gladys could learn to jump,'' Seth suggested.

Foster shuddered. ''Not again. My heart couldn't take it.''

The old man started the pickup, gunned the engine, and the battered truck lurched out onto the country road, gaining speed, until it disappeared into the early morning haze.